"Get down! Someone's shooting at us!"

The crack of a shot sent Elle flat to the ground to the right of the phone booth's concrete pad. "Henderson!"

"I'm okay," he called from his position in front of the booth. He slithered onto the dirt as more bullets decimated the remaining glass in the booth.

"Maybe we should make a run for the car?" She raised her head in time to see the windshield explode. "Or maybe not."

"I think the shooter is diagonally across the road in that orchard." He pointed in that direction as another bullet thunked into the car. "We might be able to lose him in the field and hope he doesn't follow."

The car sank down on one side as the shooter took out a tire. Another pop convinced her the field offered a better chance of survival than staying here.

"On the count of three, we'll make a run for it." Henderson's calm voice gave her the strength to gather her feet underneath her as a bullet hit the ground inches from her body. "One, two, three!"

Sarah Hamaker has nonfiction and romantic suspense books published as well as stories in Chicken Soup for the Soul volumes. She's a member of ACFW; ACFW Virginia Chapter; and Faith, Hope and Love; as well as the president of Capital Christian Writers Fellowship. Her podcast, *The Romantic Side of Suspense*, can be found on sarahhamakerfiction.com. Sarah lives in Virginia with her husband, four children and three cats.

Books by Sarah Hamaker

Love Inspired Suspense

Dangerous Christmas Memories
Vanished Without a Trace

Visit the Author Profile page at LoveInspired.com.

VANISHED
WITHOUT A TRACE

SARAH HAMAKER

LOVE INSPIRED SUSPENSE
INSPIRATIONAL ROMANCE

LOVE INSPIRED® SUSPENSE
INSPIRATIONAL ROMANCE

ISBN-13: 978-1-335-72322-2

Recycling programs for this product may not exist in your area.

Vanished Without a Trace

Copyright © 2022 by Sarah Hamaker

For questions and comments about the quality of this book, please contact us at CustomerService@Harlequin.com.

Love Inspired
22 Adelaide St. West, 41st Floor
Toronto, Ontario M5H 4E3, Canada
www.LoveInspired.com

Printed in U.S.A.

For thus saith the Lord God; Behold, I, even I,
will both search my sheep, and seek them out.
—*Ezekiel* 34:11

ONE

Henderson Parker stapled the last flyer onto a telephone pole on the outskirts of Twin Oaks. Helena's lovely face stared back at him, the mischief in her brown eyes conjuring up memories of playing hide-and-seek on Martha's Vineyard in the summer and building snow forts in the winter. Helena had been born three months after his adoption, the two of them growing up like twins. Her disappearance weighed heavily on his shoulders. If only he'd paid more attention to her, maybe he would have had a clue as to her whereabouts.

For nine years, he'd tracked down every lead, no matter how slim, in the hope it would lead to his sister, who he'd last seen in their hometown of Buffalo, New York, outside the courthouse. Even now, he could picture her sassy wave as she'd slipped into a friend's van and been driven away. Because Helena often went weeks without contact with her family, it had been nearly six months before they'd realized she had vanished. By the time Henderson had begun asking questions as to where she'd gone, the trail had grown cold.

Trudging back to his vehicle, he climbed in and cranked the engine. Deciding to let the AC cool off the interior before driving back to the B and B, he pulled out the photo that had driven him to Virginia. Like most small-town papers, the *Twin Oaks Gazette* featured the life and events of its residents. In the July 20 edition, pictures of the town's annual Christmas in July parade graced the front page and an inside spread. One of the crowd pictures had a woman with her face half turned from the camera—the resemblance to Helena was unmistakable. His first glimmer of hope in nine long years.

Arriving in Twin Oaks two days ago, he'd showed Helena's picture all around town, but no one had seen anyone who resembled her. He'd also looked over the *Gazette* photographer's other parade pictures, but could find no others with that same woman. Yesterday, he'd had a thousand flyers printed and then spent the morning putting up half of them all over the town's quaint Main Street, with its variety of shops and restaurants interspersed with city hall and a U.S. Post Office.

Drumming his fingers on the steering wheel, he contemplated his next move. Time to go to the county sheriff's department to see if they would open an investigation into Helena's disappearance now that Henderson had proof she could be in Virginia. He put the SUV in gear then glanced at his grungy attire. No one would take him seriously if he showed up in board shorts and a sweaty T-shirt. Better shower first and change into something more respectable.

He headed to Tall Trees B and B. Once inside the Federal-style mansion, he bounded up the stairs to his room, which overlooked the back gardens. Fishing in his pocket for his key—the bed-and-breakfast handed out metal keys instead of plastic keycards—he paused outside the door, noting the latch hadn't fully caught. Maybe the cleaning staff hadn't finished his room yet.

Pushing the door open, he stepped inside. At the dresser, a man wearing a baseball cap was rifling through a drawer with gloved hands.

"Hey! What are you doing?" Henderson charged toward the intruder.

The man whipped around, his eyes flaring wide above a mask obscuring the lower part of his face. Shoving away from the dresser, the intruder rammed Henderson in a full body tackle, sending him crashing into the four-poster bed. His head thwacked against one of the bedposts. Before he could recover from the exploding pain, the man punched him hard in the middle then dashed for the door.

Gasping for breath, Henderson pushed to his

knees and snagged the man's heel, bringing him down with a satisfying thud. The intruder kicked out with his other foot, catching Henderson's midsection with enough force to loosen his grip.

The man scrambled out of the room.

Shaking off the pain, Henderson staggered to the door, slumping slightly against the jamb to clear his head before going after the man. Rounding the stair landing, something hard and wet struck the side of his face, sending him back against the wall. A vase shattered beside him, raining glass and flower stems onto the carpet.

The slamming of the front door propelled him to his feet.

Henderson raced down the stairs, wrenching the door open. On the paver stone walkway, the masked intruder grappled with a woman, who delivered a well-timed head butt that aligned the top of her head with the man's nose. Blood soaked his camouflaged neck gaiter. Henderson headed toward the pair as the man growled like a wounded bear, punched the woman in the head and then spun her directly into Henderson.

Catching the woman's arms, Henderson tried to move her aside as gently as he could, but his feet tangled with hers and the two of them landed hard in the flower bed bordering the walkway. Brushing her hair off his beard, Henderson craned his neck around the woman in time to see the intruder yank a motorbike out of the bushes near the gravel parking lot. Gunning the engine, gravel spewed as the man raced off.

Henderson restrained the impulse to smash his fist into something as frustration at losing the intruder roiled inside him. Glaring at the woman still in his grip, his eyes softened. It wasn't her fault she'd foiled the capture.

"Sorry about that."

Her melodious voice had a familiar tone to it. She squirmed to extract herself from his embrace, her elbow connecting with his ribs in the same place the man's foot had collided.

Henderson grunted as pain radiated throughout his body. He rose on his elbows then rolled her slightly to the side to allow him to sit up. "Now I'm out of range of your elbows."

She pushed to a seated position, her back to him. Mulch and broken flowers entwined her brown hair. He plucked a piece out, inadvertently tugging a couple of strands of hair with it.

"Ouch." Her hand touched her head. She twisted to spear him with eyes the color of a cloudless summer day.

Warmth crept up the back of his neck over taking such a liberty with a pretty stranger. "You've got mulch in your hair."

"I do?" She finger-combed her hair, sending bits of flower and mulch flying.

His body protested rising as new aches made themselves known. Holding out his hand to the woman, he grasped hers and helped extricate her from the flower bed onto the sidewalk.

She thanked him then brushed off the back of her skirt. "Who was that guy?"

Henderson frowned. "I don't know. I found him in my room, going through my dresser."

Her eyes rounded. "How did he get into your room?"

"The locks aren't exactly state of the art."

Isabella Stratman, one of the owners of Tall Trees B and B, hurried toward them from across the lawn. "What happened?" A wide-brimmed hat shielded her face and she carried a basket of cut flowers.

"There was an intruder in Mr. Parker's room," the woman volunteered. "He raced away on a motorbike, after attacking Mr. Parker and pushing me down."

Henderson gaped. How had she known his name? To his knowledge, he'd never met her, although there was something about her voice that niggled the back of his mind. Before he could question her, Isabella spoke.

"That's terrible. Did you call 9-1-1?"

The woman shook her head. "Not yet, but we should report it." She turned to Henderson. "I didn't see anything in his hands when he rushed me. Was anything taken?"

He flashed back to the altercation. "I haven't

checked, but I can't think where he'd have put it. He was wearing jeans, boots, and a T-shirt."

"And a baseball cap and one of those neck-face covering things," the woman added.

Isabella gave each of them the once-over. "You're both hurt. You should go to the town clinic in case you have a concussion."

"I'm fine." He waved away her concern although his ribs ached and his head throbbed. "I don't understand why he was searching my room."

"I'm calling the sheriff's office now." Isabella hurried up the stairs and into the house, leaving Henderson and the woman alone.

He sucked in a breath and nearly choked as pain flared across his midsection. He touched his face, but the vase hadn't broken the skin.

"You should get ice on your head."

Placing a hand on his side, he pointed to her knees, now oozing blood from multiple lacerations. "You look like you could use some medical attention yourself."

She glanced down at her legs, a grimace twisting her lips. "Yeah, I might at that. Didn't realize I'd scraped them so badly. Guess the adrenaline is wearing off."

That was an understatement. His own body sagged and the pounding at the back of his skull ratcheted up a notch. His side ached, but he didn't think his ribs were broken. He'd cracked them playing football in high school and had never forgotten the fiery pain of each breath.

"You okay?" The woman touched his arm, concern evident in her gaze.

"Yeah, just need some ibuprofen to take care of this monster headache." His hand went to the back of his head, tender from the encounter with the bedpost. "I'm sorry you got hurt."

"It's only some scrapes."

He pointed to her face, where redness flared along her temple. "You'll probably have a nice bruise later on. Better get some ice on it."

Her fingers touched the area. "I'm sure Isabella has a cold pack in the freezer. Good thing we're currently the only guests." A smile crossed her face, bringing a sparkle to her blue eyes. "It could be awkward explaining our appearance."

He took in her rumpled shirt and skirt, bits of mulch clinging to the soft flowery material. "Except for the knees, you don't look so bad." He immediately wanted to bite his tongue. Just what every woman wanted to hear. He'd chase her off before he'd had a chance to get to know her—and he found himself hoping he hadn't because there was something about her that intrigued him.

"Thanks." A look of unease crossed her face.

He'd made her uncomfortable. "I'm sorry. I didn't mean to—"

"It's not that." The sparkle in her eyes dimmed. His body tingled with anticipation as it did whenever he sensed a witness on the stand was about to drop a bombshell he hadn't been expecting. "What is it then?"

"I know who you are, but you don't know who I am." She lowered her gaze.

Her statement reminded him of his surprise that she knew his name. He folded his arms, waiting for her to introduce herself.

"I'm Elle Updike."

Her name rang a bell, but it took him a moment to place it. Then disbelief, followed quickly by anger, infused him. "You're that podcaster who wanted to do a show on Helena's disappearance."

"That's right."

The confirmation fueled his ire. Her presence now became suspect. "Are you following me?"

"No…well, not exactly." She shifted on the paver stones, still avoiding eye contact.

"I think you need to explain."

That brought her head up to meet his stare. "I came to Twin Oaks to chase another lead for the third season of *Gone*, but…" Her voice trailed off.

"Go on," he prompted. He couldn't believe she had the audacity to try once again to convince him to let her tear Helena's life apart for entertainment.

Elle squared her shoulders. "I also knew you would be here, following up on a new lead to Helena's whereabouts."

He firmed his mouth. Only one place she could

have learned that tidbit, but he had to hear it from her lips. "How did you know that?"

"Your mother told me."

"If I find you've been hounding her…" The half-finished threat shot out of him like a bullet.

From the paleness of her cheeks, it had struck home with the force he'd intended. "Your mother chose to keep in touch. She told me about your discovery and trip to Virginia."

"I see." Anger that Elle would take advantage of his mother's continued grief over losing her daughter and more recently her husband rose, but he tamped it down with an effort. He'd learned long ago not to trust journalists; not to give them anything they could twist to their own ends. Look at how they'd painted him as the villain in that case last year involving a popular youth soccer coach who had been abusing his young players— until the overwhelming evidence had pointed to the coach's guilt and eventual conviction.

Not to mention how much trash they printed about his sister.

"Mr. Parker, please. Let me help you find Helena. Your mom said you have a photo that shows Helena was here a few months ago."

He shook his head at her sincerity, ignoring the voice telling him not to overreact. "You people don't know when to stop. I do not want your help, nor do I want you to rip my sister's life apart for your listeners' enjoyment."

"It's not like that. I can help."

He dismissed her words with a slash of his hand. Her plea might be genuine, but no way would he allow a journalist to portray his sister in an unflattering light.

"Stay away from me, Ms. Updike, or I'll have you arrested for harassment."

Elle allowed her shoulders to slump at the harshness of Henderson's response. She'd expected it would be difficult to get him to agree to the podcast, but she hadn't anticipated such vitriol regarding journalists. Then again, perhaps she'd not look kindly on reporters if they'd written such titillating stories about her sister before and after her disappearance.

"Don't worry, Mr. Parker. I understand your position and will give you a wide berth." Knowing when to retreat and when to press came in handy when dealing with troublesome sources.

Her acquiescence appeared to appease him, as his jaw relaxed slightly.

"But that might prove impossible," she continued.

Her words brought a spark of anger back to his brown eyes. "Why is that?"

She gestured toward the house. "Because I'm also a guest at Tall Trees, in the Daffodil Room, right across the hall from the Juniper Room, where you're staying." She shrugged. "It appears we are neighbors—at least for the time being. Nevertheless, I will endeavor to stay out of your way as much as possible."

"See that you do." His displeasure stamped his face in harsh lines.

An SUV pulled into the gravel lot, Shenandoah County Sheriff's Department emblazoned on the side. Elle waited silently beside Henderson as a deputy exited the vehicle and approached them.

"Good morning. I'm Deputy Barnaby Stubbs with the Shenandoah County Sheriff's Department. Mrs. Stratman said there'd been an attack and break-in."

"Thanks for responding so quickly," Henderson said.

The deputy swept his gaze over Elle and Henderson. "You two look like you caught a cat by the tail."

Isabella looked their way, then hurried down the stairs. "Deputy Stubbs, you must have been close by."

"Hey, Mrs. Stratman," Stubbs said. "I was over in Poplar about a gas station robbery."

"Was anyone hurt?" Isabella asked.

"No, and we caught the thief an hour later, high on meth."

Isabella sighed. "Mr. Parker, I thought you would be at the clinic."

"I'm fine," Henderson said in a voice that brooked no argument.

Elle could see why he was a successful prosecutor if he used that tone in court—no one would dare to oppose his statements.

Isabella stopped next to them, glancing briefly at Henderson before turning her attention to Elle. "Let's get some bandages on those scrapes."

Elle appreciated the concern. Her knees throbbed.

"Deputy," Isabella said, "you're welcome to use the front parlor to get the details from Mr. Parker. It's much too hot to stand outside and, Mr. Parker's words to the contrary, I think he needs to sit down."

With that parting shot, Isabella gently took Elle by the elbow and guided her up the stairs and into the kitchen. "Sit down on the barstool."

Elle did as directed, easing up on the padded stool, grateful for a back to lean against. This wasn't how she'd pictured approaching Henderson. Now she would have to rethink how to convince him to do the show.

Isabella pulled open the freezer drawer and grabbed a bag of frozen vegetables. "Sorry I don't have a more formal ice pack, but a guest used it last week and didn't return it. In the drawer underneath the countertop in arm's length of you, there are clean kitchen towels."

"That's okay—the veggie bag will work fine." Elle opened the drawer and extracted a towel.

"Wrap the mixed veggie bag in it for your face while I get the first-aid kit."

The cold felt good against her throbbing temple. Elle closed her eyes as the last of the adrenaline drained away, leaving her limp and exhausted. Being hit and then thrown into a flower garden hurt more than she'd thought possible, although the emotional punch of Henderson's harsh words had her reeling on the inside.

"Here we go." Isabella reentered the kitchen with a plastic bin. She bustled around the homey kitchen. The inn owner didn't speak as she gathered damp paper towels then laid out bandages, ointments and antiseptic wipes. "Okay, let's take care of your knees. Do you have any other scrapes that need bandaging?"

"No, but I can do it." Elle stretched out one leg, wincing as the movement pulled on the scrape.

"Nonsense. I'm trained in first aid. Keep those frozen veggies on your head." Isabella pulled out a barstool. "You rest while I work."

"Thanks." With a little effort, Elle swung her legs up on the stool. Mulch and dirt mingled with drying blood. "I can't remember the last time I skinned my knee."

Isabella studied the injuries as she snapped on latex gloves. "As scrapes go, these aren't too bad. I'll try not to hurt you, but I need to get the debris out."

Elle bit her lip as Isabella laid a damp paper

towel on the left knee and then gently began removing the dirt.

"Mr. Parker seemed more upset when I returned after calling the sheriff," Isabella said, her head bent over the task.

"He learned my name," Elle said, wincing as Isabella cleaned the right knee.

"He didn't like your name?"

"No…well, sort of." Elle recalled how he'd made it clear he had no respect for journalists. She'd encountered her share of those who held the media in low regard, but for some reason, hearing Henderson's opinion of reporters—of her—hurt more. "He's in town looking for his missing sister."

"Yes, I know. I helped him put up some flyers this morning." Isabella finished with the initial cleansing. She ripped open an alcohol wipe. "This is going to sting."

She wasn't kidding. The antiseptic wipe on her wounds brought tears to Elle's eyes.

"All done." Isabella bunched up the used wipes on top of the paper towels then dabbed ointment on the wounds. "He's looking for his sister and you have a podcast that looks for missing persons. Sounds like a win-win for both of you."

"You would think so, but Henderson Parker wants nothing to do with me or *Gone Without a Trace* because he thinks I would paint his sister in a poor light."

"That's too bad."

"I agree." She prided herself on being professional, on being fair and honest in her reporting. To have him assume she would not treat his sister's background with respect, hurt. To not give her a chance to prove she could be an asset in his own search, rankled. However, if their situations had been reversed, Elle would have jumped at the chance for help in finding a lost sibling. Apparently, his concern for his family's reputation outweighed accepting her offer. She hadn't pegged him as prideful, but perhaps there was more to it than a personal encounter with an overzealous reporter who pushed the boundaries of good taste in pursuit of a story.

"Star Wars or Toy Story."

Elle frowned. "What?"

Isabella waved bandages in front of her face. "Do you want a Star Wars or Toy Story bandage?"

"Oh, Star Wars."

Isabella applied the bandages and stepped back. "All done." After clearing away the first-aid items, she set a glass of water and a bottle of ibuprofen in front of Elle. "I also have aspirin or acetaminophen if you'd prefer one of those instead."

"No, this is good." Elle shook out a couple of pills then downed them with the water. "Thank you. You've gone above and beyond."

Waving her hand, Isabella smiled. "No worries. I'm happy to help."

"Mrs. Stratman?" The deputy entered the kitchen, pinching the corner of a piece of paper between his forefinger and thumb. "Do you have a plastic bag? I'm not driving my usual cruiser, so don't have any evidence bags."

Isabella handed a zip-topped bag to Stubbs. As the deputy put the piece of paper inside the bag, Henderson appeared in the doorway, his complexion pale despite the beard covering the lower half of his face.

"Mr. Parker, come, sit. You look done in." Isabella cajoled him into sitting at the round table tucked into a breakfast nook, then fetched the ibuprofen bottle and a glass of water. "Your head must be aching."

"Thank you." Henderson didn't argue, which told Elle he must be feeling pretty rotten. The man had been so testy with her earlier, she hadn't pressed him to seek help for his injuries.

"Would you walk me through the security here at the B and B?" Stubbs addressed Isabella.

"All the guest rooms have keys, and our private quarters on the third floor are kept locked as well." Isabella pulled her lips into a tight line. "But when guests are in residence, we don't keep the front door locked because one of us is always on the property."

The deputy raised his eyebrows.

Elle couldn't imagine living in a town where one didn't lock doors. She'd grown up in a home surrounded by iron fencing, a gated and locked entryway, and a state-of-the-art security system.

"Alec and I have discussed getting one of those keypad door locks but—" she turned her palms up "—the crime rate in Twin Oaks is so low, we keep putting it off."

"Putting what off?" Alec Stratman poked his head into the kitchen, several grocery bags in his hands. "Has something happened?"

Isabella quickly caught her husband up on the events of the morning. "The deputy was just asking about our security here."

"So anyone could enter the inn," Stubbs concluded.

"Yes, but you can bet that will change pronto." Alec set the bags on the counter.

"Was anything taken from Mr. Parker's room?" Elle interjected.

"No, but someone left him a message." Stubbs showed Elle the paper inside the plastic bag.

"That is a missing persons flyer about his sister…" she began when the deputy turned it over.

In red lettering that streaked down the page were the words "Go Home, Yankee."

Someone didn't want Henderson looking for his sister, but that wouldn't stop Elle from doing everything she could to ensure the Parkers had their happy ending with Helena.

TWO

At the kitchen table, Henderson rested his head in his hands, waiting for the pain reliever to take the edge off the pounding. Finding the message in his room had troubled him. Someone didn't want him looking for Helena here, which meant his sister had been or was still nearby. Nothing had been taken from his room. It appeared he had surprised the intruder before he had gone beyond the top drawer of the dresser, as only that part of his room had showed signs of disarray.

"Mr. Parker?"

At the deputy's inquiry, Henderson raised his head.

"I highly recommend you stop by the clinic," Stubbs said. "I'll take this flyer back to the office and have our lab run it for prints. Since the intruder wore gloves, I don't think we'll find anything."

"What about opening an investigation into my sister's disappearance?"

Stubbs shook his head. "I'm sorry, but there's not enough evidence to show your sister ever was in Twin Oaks. I'll give you a copy of my report to pass on to the police department in Buffalo."

"The photo from the Christmas in July parade shows she was here a couple of months ago," he protested, knowing it wouldn't be enough.

"You said so yourself that you weren't one hundred percent sure the woman in that photo is your sister," Stubbs said. "I wish we had a deputy assigned to missing persons, but we don't. Every spare officer is working on figuring out who's pouring meth into our county."

"No news on that front?" Alec asked.

"We had another death yesterday. A young woman left a husband behind." The deputy's eyes saddened. "Unfortunately, we've always had a few deaths related to drug overdoses, but these seem to be from a bad batch of meth."

"Isn't that the sixth one since July?" Alec balled the plastic grocery bags up in his hand.

"Seventh," Stubbs corrected. "And we're no closer to finding the source than we were with the first one."

"That's awful."

Elle's comment drew Henderson's attention to her. Sitting on one of the barstools with her feet propped up on the opposite stool and Star Wars bandages on her knees, she looked younger than her thirty-three years. When she had first approached his parents about making Helena's disappearance the focal point of the *Gone Without a Trace* podcast, he'd run a background check on her. Even now, her affluent upbringing surprised him. She didn't exude the privilege most wealthy children wore like a mantel. In fact, she had taken her grandmother's maiden name as her last name, going so far as to make it her legal name. That had intrigued him enough to dig deeper, but no whiff of scandal touched her or her parents. By all accounts, she had a cordial relationship with them, albeit a distant one. In the dozens and dozens of photographs he'd found of Jay and Cecily Zeller, Elle had appeared in only a handful.

"Mr. Parker—" Stubbs stuck out his hand "—we'll be in touch if anything can be lifted from the flyer. In the meantime, be careful."

"Thanks, Deputy." Henderson shook his hand.

"I'll walk you out," Alec said to the deputy. "Isabella, would you call the locksmith and see if he can work us in today?"

"Sure." Isabella followed her husband and Stubbs from the kitchen, leaving Henderson alone with Elle.

Elle hopped down from the stool, crossing to stand next to the table. "You don't look so hot at the moment."

Her words brought heat to his face as the thought she might otherwise find him attractive flitted through his mind. "I'm going to take a shower."

His mother would have a word or two to say about his rudeness, but he didn't care. He needed to distance himself from this blue-eyed woman who was bent on poking her nose into his business for the sake of entertainment. But if she hadn't been a reporter, he might have lingered to talk with her more.

The next morning, Elle dawdled in her room, hoping Henderson had already left for the day. She'd stuck mostly to her room after the incident yesterday and had managed to avoid running into him again. Cowardly of her, but she hoped to have some concrete evidence of Helena's presence in Twin Oaks as bait to persuade him to do the show. She'd spent the time yesterday posting pictures of Helena on the area social media sites, like the town's Facebook page, to see if anyone recalled seeing her around town.

Around nine, her stomach growled, a reminder that breakfast would stop being served soon. After packing her shoulder bag, she took the steps two at a time to the dining area. Her shoulders relaxed at the site of an empty room. She filled her plate with French toast, whole fresh strawberries, and crisp bacon, then sat at the small table in a tiny alcove near a floor-to-ceiling window that overlooked the rose garden.

"Good morning." Isabella breezed into the room, a large serving tray in her hands. "Did you get enough to eat?" She set the tray near the sideboard.

Elle saluted the innkeeper with her cup. "Yes, it was delicious. And excellent coffee."

"Alec started roasting his own beans, and he's finally gotten the hang of it. We're thinking of selling the whole beans in our gift shop." Isabella began dismantling the food warmers.

"You have a gift shop?" Elle didn't recall seeing such a room when Isabella had given her a quick tour Sunday night upon her arrival.

"Not yet. We hope to add one as soon as I can finalize an agreement with a few shops in town to stock their merchandise."

"I think it's a wonderful idea," Elle said.

Isabella removed her plate and silverware. "Want a warm-up on the coffee?"

"Better not." Elle added her cup to the tray. "Has Mr. Parker been down for breakfast?"

"He ate around eight fifteen then left." Isabella finished loading the tray. "What are your plans for the day?"

"Good question." No one had responded to her social media posts about Helena yet. "Try to talk to some of the townspeople, I suppose."

Isabella wiped the sideboard down with a damp cloth. "I thought Mr. Parker said he wasn't interested in doing the program?"

"He's not." Elle groaned. "But my editor most definitely is, so I need to convince him I'm not a big bad journalist, but someone who can truly help in his search for his sister."

"And finding some fresh information on Helena's whereabouts—if she's actually in the area—would go a long way to wearing down his resistance."

"Exactly." And would help her keep her job.

"Why don't you try Betsey's Beauties? I've always found salons to be hotbeds of gossip."

Elle considered the suggestion. "I could use a trim."

Isabella shook her head. "I think you should get highlights too."

Understanding dawned. "More time to talk to other customers."

"While waiting under the hair dryer for the highlights to set," Isabella added, her eyes twinkling.

"Do I need an appointment?" Elle slung her bag across her body.

"Probably not on a Tuesday, but I'd go now while it's still early. The shop is only a short block from here—it's sandwiched between the hardware store and the five-and-dime on Main Street."

"You don't have to tell me twice." Elle waved goodbye and set off, last night's storm having marginally cooled things well enough that the sun's rays pleasantly warmed her.

Betsey's Beauties had a caricature of a 1950s housewife adorning the striped awning. Pushing open the door, she found the small shop crowded with hair stylists and customers. A short hallway connected the space with the nail salon next door.

"May I help you?"

Elle nodded at the older woman with silver hair cut in an asymmetrical style that perfectly suited her angular face. "Yes, I was hoping you might be able to fit me in for a highlight and cut."

The woman studied Elle's hair, a frown pulling the lines of her forehead together over her nose. "How long have you had that style?"

Elle's cheeks warmed as she reached up to touch her hair. "It's been a while."

The woman considered Elle a moment longer. "You're much too pretty to let your hair go. Wait here."

Elle blinked at the borderline rude statement as the woman walked away.

"Excuse me."

Elle turned to see a younger woman, her shoulder-length blond hair attractively streaked with a rainbow of pastel colors, sweeping the area and needing Elle to move. She stepped out of the way while the employee whisked her broom around the floor.

"Don't take it personally. That's just Betsey's

way." The younger woman smiled. "She's the owner and a genius when it comes to hair—and she's not afraid to say it."

"Doesn't pull any punches, you mean." Elle smiled back to take the sting out of her own words.

"Takes a little getting used to, but she has a heart of gold. Goes to the assisted living place down the road every week to give free haircuts or styles to the residents."

"Jenny, please stop gabbing and get to work," Betsey said as she came back to the front desk. "The towels are piling up."

"I'm on it," Jenny said, giving Elle a wink as she scurried toward the back of the room.

Betsey assessed Elle. "Come on. We have a lot of work to do."

Elle winced, echoes of her mother's comments about her not keeping up with her appearance flooding her mind. She followed Betsey to a salon chair then patiently waited until the stylist had everything set up to begin adding the highlights. For the next half hour, Elle listened as Betsey extolled the virtues of Twin Oaks. Tucking Elle into a bank of chairs on the side, Betsey left.

"I see Betsey took you in hand," said the elderly woman sitting to Elle's right.

"Yes, she's quite a force of nature," Elle said.

The older woman chuckled. "That's an accurate way of describing her. You're new in town."

"Yes, ma'am." Elle smiled and held out her hand. "Elle Updike."

"Sally Greenhow. Your husband and kids off hiking?"

"No husband or kids. Just me."

"Boyfriend?"

Elle shook her head.

"That's a shame. A lovely girl like you ought to be married with a passel of kids."

"Everything in God's timing." She didn't mention the long line of eligible men her mother had pushed her to meet after Elle graduated from college. Those encounters generally lasted anywhere from ten minutes to one dinner, depending on the ambitions of the young man. Her father had a reputation for a keen eye on startup companies that made it and investing in the same, thus Elle often found herself at dinner with someone more interested in her father's attention than her own. It became easier to stop accepting any invitation than to spend the entire date wondering if the man opposite saw her as the means to an end.

"Amen to that," Sally replied. "You don't appear to be the typical tourist, so what brings you to Twin Oaks?"

Just the opening Elle had been waiting for. "I'm a podcast journalist—" she began.

But before she could continue, Sally jumped in. "I love listening to podcasts. My eyes aren't so good anymore, so watching TV or reading can be difficult. But I never miss an episode of *This American Life* and *Stuff You Missed in History Class*. What's your podcast called?"

"*Gone Without a Trace.* I take a cold missing persons case and investigate it, with the hope that by the final episode, we've reunited the person with the family or brought closure to them."

Sally's eyes brightened. "You must be in town to find Helena Parker."

Elle's pulse increased. "What makes you say that?"

"Well, dear, there are missing persons posters all over town. Her brother put them up."

"Do you know anything about Helena Parker being in Twin Oaks?"

"I wish I did," Sally said.

"Miss Sally, time to check your hair." Another stylist raised the hair dryer then bent over Sally, her fingers nimbly undoing one of the tiny foils on the older woman's head. "It's time for your rinse and shampoo."

Sally used the chair's armrest to assist in standing, the salon cape billowing around her slender frame. She leaned toward Elle. "If I were you, I'd ask around at the compound. Something's not right at that place, mark my words."

Elle's focus shifted to Jenny, who was sweeping up hair trimmings nearby. The young woman's posture was stiff, as if she'd been eavesdropping on their conversation and hadn't approved. Elle tucked that insight away and scrolled through her social media feeds until Betsey returned to finish the highlight and cut.

An hour later, Elle stepped onto the sidewalk, her brown hair subtly streaked with lighter shades. Betsey had cut her hair into soft layers, allowing the slight natural curl in Elle's hair to "bounce into fetching waves," as the stylist had put it. Stopping to admire her new look in the window of the hardware store, Elle caught a glimpse of Henderson coming out of the café across the street.

She wanted concrete evidence of how she could help find his sister but an older woman's cryptic words about a compound wouldn't be enough. With a sigh, she turned to walk back to the B and B to fire up her laptop for more internet sleuthing on the national missing persons websites.

Stepping away from the window, she crashed into someone on her left. "I'm sor—" Elle swallowed the rest of her apology.

The man, wearing a baseball cap pulled low over his eyes, crowded closer. A jarring tug on the strap of her bag sent Elle stumbling backward. She twisted her body away, but he tugged on the band even harder.

"Help!" She jammed her foot into the man's instep, but the self-defense move did not deter him. One explosive shove from him sent her crashing into a display of mums. The buckle holding the strap to her bag snapped. Elle quickly wrapped the loose band around her hand and hung on as he yanked. She screamed again as he swung one of his boot-clad feet at her head.

Elle flung a hand over her head and braced for the blow.

THREE

Henderson twisted off the lid on his steaming cup of coffee and flung the cup's contents at Elle's attacker. Hot liquid burst out of the container and down the man's back. Good thing he'd spotted Elle when exiting the coffee shop across the street and realized she was in trouble.

With a yell, the man writhed, his fingers pulling the damp fabric away from his skin. His eyes met Henderson's. In that instant, Henderson recognized the man as the one from the inn attack. Then the man bolted.

Henderson tore off after him, legs pumping. The man darted across a side street, Henderson gaining on him. On the next block, a tourist bus had pulled up in front of the Christmas in Your Heart boutique. The man slipped past the bus as the doors opened and the passengers disembarked. Henderson wove around the chattering women but one bumped into him with her enormous bag, knocking him off balance enough that he stumbled.

By the time he regained his feet, the man had disappeared. Frustration bubbled up like a volcano.

Someone touched his arm and he whirled around. Elle stood by his side, hugging her bag. "Did you lose him?"

"Yes." Her words rankled him but he wouldn't let on. He eyed the milling women now filling the entire sidewalk in front of the shop. "The tourists got in my way."

She sighed. "Was it the same man from yesterday?"

"I think so. The eyes certainly looked the same, but yesterday he was wearing a gaiter in addition to the baseball cap." He frowned, dragging up the memory of the man who'd attacked them. "But the cap was different. Yesterday, he wore a John Deere tractor cap. Today, it was one with a fishing logo of some sort. Didn't catch the name."

"Fishers of Men," Elle supplied, "with a fish symbol and a line with a hook dangling from the mouth of the fish. Do you think we should report it to the sheriff's office, since we think it's the same man?"

"I suppose. I'll call Stubbs and tell him what happened." He pulled out his wallet, extracting the deputy's card.

Elle waited beside him while he relayed the

morning's events to the deputy. Stubbs wasn't convinced it was the same man as the day before, but said he would add the report to the break-in file. Henderson thanked the man and hung up.

"He said since nothing was taken and no one was hurt, he would come by the B and B later today or tomorrow to take your statement, as he's headed out to a three-car pileup on the highway," he said.

She nodded. "Do you know if any of the businesses have exterior security cameras?"

He shook his head. "They don't. I asked when I put up the flyers. The city council felt they would be too off-putting to tourists, making it seem like the town's not safe."

"Maybe I've been living in the big city for far too long to believe any place is truly safe."

Her words reminded him to tread carefully to not reveal he'd delved into her background. "What big city is that?"

"Washington, DC," she said, rushing on as if she didn't want to reveal more personal details. "Don't you think it's strange that the same man tried to mug me after searching your room yesterday?"

He let her change the subject, since she had voiced the very question he had. "I do, but Stubbs doesn't."

"Why not?"

"As he mentioned yesterday, there's been an influx of meth in the area, and crime has been up, even in small towns like Twin Oaks. He thinks it was just a weird coincidence of you being the wrong place at the wrong time today. You said so yourself that the street appeared to be deserted when you left the salon."

"Yeah, I suppose that could be the case." She rearranged her arms around the purse. "Anyway, I need to either get another bag or have this strap fixed." She pointed to a dry cleaner's store across the street. "I think I see a spool and thread symbol, so hopefully there's a tailor on the premises who can repair this."

Henderson followed her across the street, not asking himself why he felt compelled to make sure she was okay after her attempted mugging. The dry cleaner did have a tailor shop tucked inside with a tiny older woman busily hemming pants at a sewing machine. She clucked her tongue while examining Elle's purse, but declared she could fix the strap. Elle dumped the contents into a plastic grocery bag, tied it off, and left the purse behind the counter after extracting her wallet, phone and a leather-bound book secured with a band.

On the sidewalk outside the shop, Henderson took his first bite of humble pie. "Can I buy you a coffee?"

She raised her eyebrows. "You're willing to

drink with the enemy? Besides, I should be the one buying you a cup for coming to my rescue."

She wasn't going to make this easy. He blew out a breath. "Look, I'm sorry I was less than gracious yesterday after learning your name."

Elle didn't answer, her blue eyes fixed on his as if expecting more of an explanation, which he'd reluctantly tackle.

"A little of my family history might be helpful." He swallowed hard. "Helena and I grew up like twins because of our close birthdays. We were in the same grade at school, and always looked out for one another. Until high school, when Helena began clashing more with our father." No matter how many times Henderson had asked his sister about the rift, she'd refused to give him a straight answer.

"Helena ran around with a wild crowd and, after graduation, she continued partying hard and dropped out of community college after the first semester." He paused. "What I'm trying to say is that I don't want the only thing people remember about my sister is the drugs and partying. She was more than that."

"Do you think something happened to push her onto that path?"

"Maybe." He extended an olive branch. "My mother wants to do the show, and I'm willing to go along if I have your word that you won't paint

Helena only as a party girl, that you'll show her sweet side too."

Elle bit her lower lip, a gesture he was beginning to equate with her "thinking" pose. "I always try to give a balanced view of the missing person and their families. I can't promise more than that."

"Then let's get that coffee and talk strategy," he said, leading the way to the café and praying he hadn't made the wrong bargain.

Elle settled into the booth while Henderson ordered their coffees at the counter. He'd politely insisted on paying for their drinks. She quickly sent a text to her podcast editor, Caren.

Landed the fish! Starting background interview with HP now.

Caren's reply popped up immediately.

I knew you could do it. Emailing the new program info sheet from the network—need it filled out & sent back pronto. I already asked Sabina to start combing the web for news articles on the Parker family. Don't get distracted by Mr. Handsome.

Elle frowned. Caren sometimes pushed the envelope too far when discussing an interview subject's physical appearance, so Elle chose to ignore the last comment. The show's researcher,

Sabina, had the ability to ferret out all kinds of information, leaving Elle to concentrate on the interviews.

"One iced mocha with caramel drizzle." Henderson set her frothy drink down, a cup of coffee in his other hand. "Since it's straight-up noon, I also took the liberty of ordering us the lunch special—crab and onion quiche with a side of spring greens."

"Sounds delicious, thank you." She sipped the cold beverage, allowing the iciness of the coffee to cool her tongue. Despite last night's rain, temperatures were beginning to climb again.

"How does this work?" Henderson lifted his own cup to his well-shaped lips.

Caren's "Mr. Handsome" comment drifted through her mind. Her producer was right—Henderson Parker could grace the cover of *GQ* with his warm brown eyes and stylishly cut brown hair brushed up on the top, the sides short. A neatly trimmed beard hugged the rugged curves of his strong jawline.

But she wasn't there to admire her subject—she had a job to do, and she'd better get her mind in the game. "I'd like to go over some background of the case, then hear what's happened in the two years since I originally approached your family about doing the podcast." She pulled out her phone. "However, you'll need to sign a waiver before we begin. It's online, so I'll text you the link."

Henderson rattled off his number and she sent the link. While he filled out the online form, their food arrived.

"Smells delicious." Elle picked up her fork.

"Hold on." He smiled and extended his hand, palm up. "Mind if I say a blessing?"

Without giving herself time to debate the merits of holding his hand even for a quick prayer, she grasped his and bowed her head.

"Dear Heavenly Father, please bless our lunch and help us to find my sister. Amen."

With a gentle squeeze, he returned to his phone. "You go ahead and get started. I'm almost finished reading the waiver."

"You must be a lawyer. Everyone else skims it and signs it at the bottom in about five seconds." She took a bite of the quiche, the flaky crust a perfect complement to the well-cooked filling.

He tapped a few times on the screen then used his finger to sign. "I should be horrified, but I can understand why. It probably doesn't make much sense if you're not an attorney."

They made small talk while finishing their lunch. Once the waiter had cleared the dishes, Elle opened her notebook. "When I spoke to Kathleen the first time, she said your dad had hired private investigators when Helena first went missing. Tell me about that."

She jotted notes as Henderson relayed what a series of PIs had not found. All had traced Helena's movements up until sometime in March nine years ago. Then the trail had gone stone cold.

"No one could figure out what happened to her after that?" As unbelievable as that sounded, Elle was all too familiar with how that could happen. People disappeared all the time without a trace, leaving behind families desperate for answers that never came.

"Nope. Not until I came across the crowd photo from the Christmas in July parade."

"How did that come about?"

"I think it must have been a God thing."

Elle cocked her head. "Why do you say that?"

"About six weeks ago, I had a Facebook friend request from someone I knew in college. Turns out his sister lives near Twin Oaks, and he'd been to visit her for the Christmas in July parade. He'd shared the *Gazette* photo because his niece was in the band featured in front of the crowd." Henderson leaned forward, his eyes intent on hers. "I never would have seen that photo hadn't my friend sent that request at just the right time."

"So you think God had something to do with that." Her parents had always talked about God as someone who had little interest in the inner workings of human beings, kind of like a benevolent ruler who sometimes rained down blessings and sometimes rained down curses on people.

But Elle had chosen to believe God cared about His creation—yet another way she didn't fit into her parents' world.

"Yes, I do." Henderson held her gaze.

"I can see why." Her concession took some of the challenge from Henderson's eyes. "Tell me why you think it's Helena in the photo."

He held out his phone, the photo displayed. "Here's the picture."

The photographer had framed the high school marching band's wind section as the focal point, with the crowd slightly blurry behind the maroon-and-gold uniforms.

Henderson pinched the screen and changed the focus, enlarging the crowd behind a flutiest until a dark-haired woman's head dominated the space. He handed her the phone. "That's Helena."

Elle studied the woman's blurry features, displayed nearly in profile. She'd taken a quick glance at the picture yesterday when Henderson had showed it to the deputy, noting the hardware store behind the crowd. But she hadn't realized which of the women Henderson had thought Helena was until now. Mentally comparing the photo from the flyer with this older woman, she couldn't see the resemblance. Maybe the entire thing was a wild-goose chase, and Helena had never been anywhere near Twin Oaks. She tamped down her disappointment. There was still enough to pursue the case for the podcast, but if she didn't find new evidence soon, Caren would pull the plug.

She passed the phone back to him. "I'll be honest. She doesn't look like Helena to me."

He slid the device back into his pocket. "It's her. I know it is."

His voice held the same implacable certainty she'd heard in family members of other missing persons. The need to know where a loved one had gone must be nearly impossible to live with, and so many of them clung to dubious claims of sightings or photographic evidence, like the parade picture, that had little basis in reality.

But Elle wouldn't be the one to tell Henderson it couldn't be Helena. He'd come to that conclusion soon enough on his own.

Her admiration for his dedication in chasing down any clue, no matter how slim, spurred her own resolve to help him however she could. Unease took up residence as she recalled the two attacks. She couldn't dismiss them as easily as the deputy did, and until she figured out how they were connected with Helena's disappearance, she would be on her guard.

FOUR

"That was harder than I thought it would be." Henderson unclipped the lavalier microphone from the collar of his polo shirt. He hadn't realized how talking about Helena's initial disappearance would impact him emotionally. There had been a few times when he'd had to clear his throat to get the words out.

"You did great." Elle efficiently coiled the wire, tucking the mic back into a small pouch along with her own. The late-afternoon sun cast long shadows across the backyard of Tall Trees, providing welcome shade and slightly cooler temperatures.

During their hour-long interview, her voice had conveyed shock, warmth and concern in turn, infusing the discussion with a personal tone that had put him at ease. "You would make a fantastic lawyer—you'd have the jury eating out of your hand."

She laughed as she finished packing the recording equipment. "No, thank you. I'll stick with my little podcast where the stakes aren't as high as finding justice."

"Aren't you being a little too modest?" In between their morning encounter and their formal interview, Henderson had researched her podcast more thoroughly. Elle, along with her editor/producer Caren Slater, had done the first season of *Gone Without a Trace* on a shoestring budget. But Elle's dogged determination and investigative reporting had uncovered new leads in a decades-old disappearance of a young Black mom who'd supposedly left her husband and three children without a word. Her persistence had uncovered Sara Levy's murderer and the location of her remains—and garnered thousands of listeners in the process.

Her hands stilled. "What do you mean by modest?"

"Your podcast isn't 'little.' You're now playing with the big boys as part of the Perfect Podcast Network. You must be anxious to make a good impression with the upcoming season."

"Yes, my podcast now has a home with PPN, but I'm still committed to bringing the same level of energy and investigation to your sister's disappearance as I did before PPN bought the rights to *Gone.*"

"I don't doubt that." He hadn't meant to imply she wouldn't work as hard on Helena's case because PPN now owned *Gone*. However, his research had also uncovered PPN's propensity for clickbait headlines, which tended to drive ratings higher. "I just hope you're not unduly influenced to spend more airtime on Helena's troubled past in search of more listeners in light of the network's reputation for pushing the envelope of good taste."

The anger flashing in her eyes clued him in that he had stuck his foot into it, when he had only wanted to express his concern that Elle might not be able to withstand pressure from PPN higher-ups to produce a more salacious show.

"If you're that worried, then perhaps you should not have agreed to do the podcast. Good day, Mr. Parker." She shouldered her bag with a new strap and stalked from the garden into the house.

Henderson sighed. That could have gone better. On the bright side, at least he'd waited to tick her off until after their interview. Part of him wanted to go after her to apologize but his more prudent side told him to stay put and let her work off the anger first. He tried not to think about how pretty she looked with ire bringing more color to her cheeks and a fire to her eyes. He had to keep focused on finding Helena and not allow himself to be distracted by thoughts of Elle on a personal level.

Glancing at his phone to note the hour, now

was as good a time as any to check his work email before finding a place to eat dinner. If he didn't sweep through his email at least once a day, it would be a snarled mess upon his return to the office.

When he rounded the stairs, he noticed Elle's door stood partially open. Maybe she'd run down to her car for a minute and hadn't closed it all the way. He put his key in his door's lock, but pulled it out again. With the search of his room fresh on his mind, he couldn't ignore the anomaly of an unclosed door.

Stepping across the hall, he knocked on the door frame. "Elle? Are you okay?"

Silence. The hairs on the back of his neck prickled. Something wasn't right. He pushed open the door. Elle's bag lay on the blanket chest at the foot of the bed, her sandals in a heap beside it. "Elle?"

A faint sob came from behind him. He turned toward the bathroom door, which was ajar. Moving cautiously, he approached the bathroom until he could peer inside. Elle stood in the middle of the floor in her bare feet, her back ramrod-straight.

"What's wrong?"

"Don't come any closer." Her words halted his forward movement.

"Why not?"

"There's…there's…" She paused and then tried

again. "There's a copperhead snake behind the toilet."

His heart pounded as Henderson scrambled to remember if that breed was venomous. "Has it seen you?"

"Yes." Her breath hitched.

"You're sure it's a copperhead?"

"I see the distinct reddish-brown crossbands saddlebag pattern. I think it's a young one, because the tail is yellowish."

He fumbled for his phone with clumsy fingers. "I'm calling 9-1-1. Don't move."

"Don't worry—I'm frozen in place."

"Nine-one-one. What's your emergency?"

Henderson relayed the situation as succinctly as possible. "What should she do?"

"Is the snake's tail vibrating?" The 9-1-1 dispatcher's calm voice brought his heart rate down slightly.

"Ma'am, I'm putting you on speaker." After pushing the button, he asked Elle the question.

"Yes, that's why I'm haven't moved."

"I've dispatched animal control and the sheriff's department. Stay still and don't threaten the snake in any way," the dispatcher said.

"I'm doing my best not to," Elle said.

"Sir, are you also within striking distance?"

"No, I'm outside the bathroom, and can't even see the snake."

"Good. Do not approach the snake or try to capture it. Stay back."

"Please hurry."

"ETA for animal control is ten minutes, with a deputy minutes behind him. You need to keep the line open until they arrive."

"Okay." Henderson lowered the phone, his attention on Elle's back. "You doing okay?"

"I'm hanging in there." Elle's voice cracked. "How long did she say?"

"About ten minutes. Why don't you tell me what happened?" He hoped talking about it might help to distract her, but what he really wanted to do was hold her close. He shouldn't be attracted to her, not when his focus should be solely on finding Helena, but something about the podcaster made him want to protect her.

"When I came in the bathroom, I saw something move behind the toilet. That's when I spotted the snake." She blew out a controlled breath.

"I've never seen one up close and personal." All he could think to do was to keep her talking while they waited for the professionals to arrive.

"This isn't my first encounter with this particular breed of snake," she volunteered. "I spent several summers in Shenandoah National Park as part of A Christian Ministry in the National Parks program. One summer, my job was helping the rangers with their outdoor programs, which included talks about wildlife. I learned how to identify snakes native to Virginia, including the copperhead. Usually, these aren't found in houses—they much prefer uninhabited areas or piles of leaves or wood."

He digested that information. "You're saying it couldn't have crawled up here on its own, so…"

"Someone had to have placed it here. On purpose," she finished.

Elle didn't take her gaze from the snake, which stayed coiled into the small space behind the toilet, its head resting at a forty-five-degree angle. Copperheads generally didn't strike unless provoked, but she noted its tail continued to vibrate, showing its agitation despite the stillness of the rest of its body. While usually not deadly, the venom caused extreme pain for days—not something she wanted to experience firsthand.

"I don't know why someone would deliberately let loose a copperhead in my room, unless…" She paused, running through her movements in sequential order. "I arrived Sunday night around nine, and went straight to bed. Monday morning, I came here hoping to talk with you."

"Instead, you were collateral damage when the intruder knocked you down after searching my room then attacking me," he interjected.

The wheels in her mind spun faster. "Today, after getting my hair highlighted and styled at the beauty salon, I was mugged."

Elle slowly rotated her stiff shoulders up and down in an attempt to ease some of the tension. Holding still was harder than it looked, but any sudden movement could trigger an attack from the snake, whose forked tongue occasionally flicked in and out. In this moment, she couldn't recall if a male snake had the longer or shorter forked tongue.

"Did you ask about Helena at the salon?"

His question refocused her attention on the conversation. "I didn't get a chance. Betsey— the owner, who also did my hair—talked a mile a minute. I did chat briefly with an older customer when we both were sitting under the hair dryers. She hadn't seen Helena but she did suggest checking out the compound outside of town. No specifics. I was going to ask Isabella and Alec about it the next time I saw them."

"A compound?"

"That's what the woman called it. She said something wasn't right there, but she didn't say what, and I didn't get a chance to ask her. Have you heard anything about it?"

"Not a thing."

"Hello?" a female voice called. "Animal Control here."

"I'll be right back," Henderson said.

Elle didn't turn around but heard his footsteps cross to the bedroom door, then his giving directions to Elle's bathroom.

"Elle, we have Deputy Stubbs and Animal Control officers here," Henderson said.

She glanced over her shoulder to see the deputy and two other officers, one holding a long stick with a metal-braided flat hook on the end and a pair of long-handled tongs, before turning back to the snake. The copperhead flicked out its long tongue, its tail vibrating.

"Hey, there. I'm Amy and this is my partner, Jake. Where's the snake?" Amy's voice had an easy confidence that helped Elle draw in a steadying breath.

"In the bathroom, behind the toilet," Henderson answered.

"Elle, I'm going to ease up behind you slowly. Just keep your eyes on the snake," Amy said.

"Okay." Elle gripped her fingers together.

"He's on the small size but the young ones still can be deadly," Amy said. "I don't want to spook him. Don't worry—I have a foolproof plan. I'll pin the snake down with my hook. Then you'll exit the bathroom. Sound good?"

"Yes." Elle held her breath while the woman expertly subdued the snake right behind its head with the flat hook.

"Okay, Jake, can you escort Elle from the room?" Amy said.

Elle jumped when Jake touched her shoulder. "You can leave now," the officer told her.

Slowly, Elle backed out of the space, nearly

tripping over her own feet. The enormity of the situation crashed down on her, and she collapsed into Henderson's arms. Pressed against him, she clung to his strength, her own gone now that the immediate danger had passed. Behind her, the murmurs of the Animal Control officers faded as she gave in to the urge to bury her face in Henderson's strong chest. His polo shirt carried the scent of cedar, and she breathed deeply.

"You're safe now," Henderson whispered. His hands rubbed up and down her back, the rhythmic motion smoothing away the terror of the last few moments.

"Got it!" Amy's declaration prompted Elle to lift her head. The woman held a five-gallon bucket with an attached lid, air holes punched in the top. "You were right—it was a copperhead, but it's contained now."

Elle shuddered. "What will you do with it?"

"Take it far into the woods and release it," Amy said.

"Any idea how it got in here?" Deputy Stubbs spoke for the first time.

"I can't tell you that, but I do know that snake didn't waltz in here on its own," the female officer said.

"Why do you say that?" Elle had come to the same conclusion but wanted to hear from an expert.

"Because it's not winter. No way a copperhead

would decide this would be a good place to hang out when there's a nice, warm, quiet forest with plenty of rocks not far away." Amy rested the end of the hook on the floor.

"Elle and I think someone must have put it in here," Henderson said.

Amy nodded. "That would be my best guess. Toilet's the closest thing to a rock, so the snake slithered on in there to hang out."

"He'll be much happier once we return him to his natural habitat," Jake added. "We'd best be off, unless you need anything else?"

If someone had deliberately released a venomous snake in her room, chances were pretty good they might have done so because of her asking about Helena. That meant Henderson could face a similar situation.

Elle stepped out of Henderson's arms, already missing the comfort. "You might want to check Henderson's room too," she said. "We both were in the garden for a while, so someone could have gotten into his room too."

"Good idea," the deputy said.

"I'll unlock the door." Henderson went across the hall while Elle collapsed on the bench at the foot of the bed.

Her heart rate still beat fast, but whether from the snake encounter or being held in the arms of a handsome man, she wasn't one hundred percent sure. What she did know for certain was that someone wasn't playing a garden-variety prank—that snake was meant to do more than simply scare her. But if Helena went missing on her own accord, as the police believed, why would someone care if she were found? Unless Helena's disappearance hadn't been voluntary after all.

FIVE

Elle had taken Isabella up on her offer of a bowl of homemade tortilla soup for dinner in her room. The spicy broth, chicken, corn, black beans and thin tortilla strips had hit the spot. Now, even though the clock displayed 8:00 p.m., she'd changed into her pajamas. A long soak in the claw-foot tub had been tempting, but she could barely face the bathroom after the earlier scare. Settling back against the headboard, a cup of tea on the end table and the latest legal thriller by her favorite author beside her, Elle willed the tranquility of her surroundings to permeate her mind.

No snake had been found in Henderson's room, nor in any other room of the inn. Isabella had arrived home while Animal Control had warily searched Henderson's room. The owner had then demanded they search the entire house. Not that Elle blamed Isabella. She'd have done the same thing for peace of mind.

A good book would have to wait. She needed

to see if Caren had sent the background information promised after Elle's text about the incident. Skimming through the email on her phone, she spotted a recent one from Caren.

Several interesting tidbits about your man in the gossip columns.

Just like Caren to start calling Henderson "her" man because he was single and handsome—and because, as Elle's friend, she wanted her to settle down with someone. Elle continued reading.

I've cut and pasted the relevant bits about HP. Quite the man about town as a young district attorney. Nothing more recent than three years ago, though. Happy hunting! Caren

The original research into the Parkers had focused on Helena, not Henderson. She pondered that for a moment before taking a sip of her herbal raspberry tea, then reading the first news item dated six years ago.

Henderson's face, minus the close-cropped beard, dominated the small screen. Below the photo, the piece entitled "Buffalo Bachelors" gave a brief bio of "one of the city's up-and-coming legal minds—and eligible bachelor—Henderson Parker." His profile read like the privileged man he was: private schools, where he was a star quarterback on the football team; Harvard law school; public defender's office for five years before switching at age thirty to the district attorney's office.

Nothing out of the ordinary there, except for his stint as a public defender. Elle made a mental note to find out why he'd made the change to prosecutor. The next article, dated four years ago, noted Henderson's engagement to Janice Whitman, a graphic artist. The two had met at a charity event and were planning a wedding the following spring.

Elle hadn't noticed a ring on Henderson's left hand, but not all married men wore wedding rings. The thought that he might be taken saddened her as the memory of his arms invaded her mind. After being so scared the snake would strike, having him rub her back and let her blubber all over his chest had erased much of the fear.

She returned to the email to read the last story, dated three years ago. It consisted of a few lines inserted in the *Buffalo Times*'s gossip column.

Good news to all you single ladies—Assistant District Attorney Henderson Parker is back on the market, as his wedding to Janice Whitman is off. What happened? Two weeks before the scheduled nuptials, the bride up and married her college sweet-

heart, Doug Browning. No comment from the groom in response to our inquiries.

How awful for Henderson. She'd never even come close to finding a man with whom marriage seemed a remote possibility, never mind making it to the engagement part. No matter which dating app she'd tried—and she'd tried several—the men did one of three things. Didn't show up at all. Showed up, ate and then left her with the bill after "going to the bathroom." Or, at the end of the meal, confessed she wasn't "attractive enough."

Her mother's voice whispered in her ear. "If you lost those ten extra pounds and wore more fashionable outfits, maybe a man would stick around for dessert."

What she'd never told her mother was that the few who did follow up after the date inevitably wanted to be introduced to her father because "they had a fledgling company he would want to invest in." Elle had tired of coming in second to her father's reputation as a startup company investor.

Shutting down that line of thinking, she sent a quick reply to Caren, thanking her for the info, then started to put down her phone when she decided to see if anything popped up when she searched for "compound" and "Twin Oaks, Virginia."

The first hit was for some sort of game-and-bar place called The Compound. Next came listings for compound bows, a campground named The Wind Family Compound, and multiple references to the Marine compound part of Camp Rapidan, the summer home of President Herbert Hoover now located in Shenandoah National Park.

A dead end.

Maybe if she added the last place Helena had been seen—Buffalo, New York—with the word "compound," she'd find a connection. The search returned listings for pharmacy compounds, a janitorial company with compound in the name, and listings of compound bows for sale. She was about to close out and pick up her book when a headline way down the page caught her attention.

"Fire at Local Compound Kills One."

She clicked on the decade-old story, dated January 12.

ERIE COUNTY—The Erie County Sheriff's Office and Fire and Rescue Department responded to a call about a fire late at night at what officials described as a "compound" located ten miles outside Buffalo. The fire burned one of the old barns on the property to the ground. No other buildings suffered damage. However, when fire investigators walked the scene the following morning, they discovered the charred remains of a body.

Obadiah Judd, listed as the owner of the

thirty-acre plot, identified the deceased as Sam Smith, a vagrant who had been given permission to sleep in the unused barn. "I warned Sam not to smoke, given the age of the structure, but I guess he didn't listen," Judd said.

A follow-up story appeared in the newspaper three weeks later.

ERIE COUNTY—The Erie County Fire and Rescue Department investigators concluded that the fire at an old barn near the Erie County line had been started as a result of burning cigarette left by a vagrant man, who died of smoke inhalation. "We believe the man, who's been identified as Sam Smith, fell asleep with a lit cigarette, which subsequently ignited moldy hay on fire," said Brad Thompson, a veteran fire investigator with the department. "We're officially ruling the fire and death accidental."

Obadiah Judd, owner of the property, asked for anyone who knew Sam to contact him. "Because he died on our property, we've given him a Christian burial, but if he has family still living, I'd like for them to know his final resting place," Judd said. The Erie County Sheriff's Office has had no luck tracking down any of Smith's relatives. *If you have information about Sam Smith, please contact the sheriff's office at 555-555-5555.*

Elle composed an email to Sabina Ackerman, *Gone*'s researcher, asking her to look into Obadiah Judd and giving her the two article links for reference. Probably a fruitless task but sometimes being thorough paid off. She closed the apps on the phone and then finished her tea before snuggling down in the bed to read.

As drowsiness began to envelop her, the sound of wind chimes tickled the edges of her consciousness. Elle blinked, bringing the room into focus. The sound registered. Fumbling in the covers, she located her cell phone, checked caller ID for the missed call, and noted the time. Kathleen Parker. Ten twenty-one. She must have fallen asleep reading. The phone rang again.

"Hello, Kathleen?"

"She called me."

Elle could barely make out the words behind Kathleen's sobbing.

"What?"

The older woman drew in a ragged breath before replying. "She called me. Helena called me."

At the certainty in Kathleen's voice, Elle's pulse jumped. Kathleen's sobs had diminished but, to Elle's ears, they weren't the result of happy tears. "I'm going to record our conversation, is that okay?"

"Yes."

Elle quickly engaged the recording app, not wanting to miss a word of what Kathleen would say. "Tell me everything."

A knock on Henderson's door drew his attention. Probably Isabella or Alec with fresh towels since his light was on, but as he crossed to the door, he also mentally braced for bad news.

Elle stood in the hall, her hair mussed. Without preamble, she pushed past him into his room, clutching her phone in her right hand. "Your mom couldn't get a hold of you, so she called me."

Henderson scooped up his phone, which had been plugged in to charge, from the bedside table. "It's dead." Then he remembered what Isabella had said about the wall socket near the bed.

He groaned. "I forgot to flip on the light switch to activate the outlet." He did so before turning back to Elle. "I'm sorry if she bothered you. Since my dad died, she sometimes gets agitated if she can't contact me right away."

"It's not that." She paced to the fireplace then back to the center of the room. "With her permission, I recorded our conversation. I think it's best if you listen first."

"Okay."

Elle tapped her phone and set it down on the

bedside table. Her voice filled the room. "Kathleen, walk me through what happened."

"About twenty minutes ago, the landline rang," his mom said, the stress in her voice making the hairs on his arms stand to attention. "I always ignore the first ring because Henderson put one of those spam filters on the phone. I used to get so many telemarketing calls. It rang once then nothing. But then it rang again and kept ringing. I checked caller ID and it said unknown with a 540 area code. I nearly let it roll to voicemail, but something made me pick up the call."

Elle gently encouraged Kathleen to continue. "I said hello, and there was a short pause before someone said, 'Mom, it's Helena.'"

His heart hammered. Even though he'd been hoping his sister would one day contact him or their mom as if she'd never been gone, the shock at hearing his mother say those words sent him staggering. He groped behind him for the ladder-backed chair next to the table and sank into it. Helena was alive and apparently well enough to phone. Yet his lawyerly side mentally questioned the validity of the caller even as Elle did the same on the recording.

"How did you know it was Helena?" Elle pressed.

"She told me the name of her imaginary friend as a preschooler. Jingle. Only Henderson and myself know that name. It was Helena."

Henderson closed his eyes, memories of playing with Helena, with Jingle in tow, as children. She'd taken her imaginary friend with her everywhere for weeks one summer.

"Where is Helena?" Elle's gentle tone appeared to soothe his mother because Kathleen's voice had calmed during the course of the conversation.

"She wouldn't say, but she told me that she was fine, and she was sorry for not keeping in touch."

"Did she say why she was calling now?"

"No, she only repeated she was okay and to not worry, and that she didn't want to come home." His mother began sobbing again. "I begged her to, but she refused."

"Did she say anything else?"

Kathleen brought her crying under control enough to reply in a clear voice. "She asked me to relay a message to Henderson."

He held his breath.

"She wanted to know if he'd remembered her favorite game as a child."

"That's all?" Elle echoed his own thought.

"Yes, she said goodbye and hung up before I could talk to her further." Kathleen's sobs abruptly halted as Elle turned off the recording.

"What do you think—was it really your sister?" Elle studied his face.

He scrubbed a hand over his beard. "My gut says yes. She's the only one besides Mom and me who would know about Jingle."

"Any clue as to why she'd ask your mother about whether you could recall the name of her favorite childhood game?"

"No. All I can remember is that most of them fixated on finding something lost." The memory of Helena dramatically informing him they were orphans searching for their missing fortune brought a smile to his lips.

Elle tensed. "That doesn't tell us much."

"That's all I can come up with for now." He rested his forearms on his knees. "What about the phone number?"

"I called it, but it just rang and rang. I sent it to my researcher to track down a possible name or location, so hopefully I'll know something by the morning."

"Wait a second—" the area code rang a bell "—540 is a local area code."

"But it could be a cell phone, so that, in and of itself, doesn't mean Helena's nearby."

"It's too much of a coincidence that we start asking around about Helena and someone claiming to be her calls my mom." He'd played enough odds in the courtroom to know coincidences like that didn't happen in real life.

"I agree." Elle's eyes met his, her gaze troubled. "If that's true, then it follows the break-in and attack on you wasn't random."

He carried the thought through to its natural

conclusion. "And neither were the mugging and snake in your room."

Her blue eyes widened. "We may have poked a hornet's nest."

"I only hope we can avoid getting stung."

SIX

The Pink Pig had only a few patrons when Elle arrived at the eatery a little before noon. A silver-haired waiter directed her to a booth in the corner, then recited the day's specials. She ordered a glass of unsweetened iced tea flavored with fresh mint leaves from the restaurant's kitchen garden. While she waited for Henderson to arrive, she scanned her social media accounts.

"Good morning." Henderson slid onto the opposite bench, his hair still damp. "Don't mind my wet hair. I grabbed a quick shower after a morning run."

The waiter appeared with her iced tea, gave Henderson a rundown of the specials, and departed with his drink order of a Kale Tonic Fresh Juice.

"That's a bold beverage choice," she said.

"Hey, I'll have you know I make a mean kale smoothie." He defended himself with a twinkle in his eye. "I couldn't pass up the chance to taste kale, apple, cucumber and lemon mixed together. Besides, I could use a tonic today."

"Rough night?"

The dark circles under his eyes revealed the answer even before he answered. "Is it that obvious?" He blew out a breath. "I kept thinking about Helena and wondering if she really called our mom."

Elle squeezed fresh lemon into her tea. "I think we should proceed as if she did."

"Continue what we're doing to find her in this area?"

She nodded as the waiter returned with a glass of water for Henderson. "Your tonic will be ready in a couple of minutes. May I take your order?"

Henderson gestured for Elle to go first.

"I'll have the Southwestern Shredded Pork Salad please, hold the tomatoes." She handed back the menu.

"I'd like the Pesto Chicken Quinoa Bowl, thanks," Henderson said.

Alone again, his expression turned serious. "I fielded a dozen calls this morning relating to the flyer."

Elle's eyebrows arched. "You don't sound happy about that."

"I'm not." He unrolled his silverware in the paper napkin, placing the knife and fork precisely on the smooth wooden tabletop and the napkin on his lap. "Not one person had information about

Helena. In fact, most only asked how much the reward was and how long it took to collect it."

"I'm sorry." She hadn't expected the flyers to generate true leads, but they did let people know he was still looking for his sister, and that could help when they talked face-to-face with residents.

The waiter served Henderson's tonic, along with their lunches. As he'd done yesterday, Henderson clasped her hand and uttered a short prayer of thanksgiving for their food.

While they ate, conversation drifted along polite lines as they chatted about the weather, their favorite sport and the latest book they'd read.

After the waiter cleared the dishes, Elle pulled out her notebook. "I found out some news about the phone number."

His brow wrinkled. "The one Helena called my mom from?"

"Yes." She consulted her notes, although she didn't need them. "Sabina—that's the podcast's researcher—traced the number to this area."

The excitement in his eyes made her stomach clench.

"That's great! Why didn't you say so immediately?" He started to scoot out of the booth. "We should check it out in person."

"Wait." Her voice halted his actions. "Before we go, I need to tell you what she found."

"Okay." He perched on the edge of the seat.

"It's a pay phone booth in the middle of nowhere."

His expression clouded with confusion, mirroring her own disbelief when she'd read Sabina's email. "A pay phone? I didn't think they still had those."

She offered a wry smile. "Apparently, they do." She pulled out her phone and opened a maps app. "Here, it's near the crossroads of routes 734 and 732, close to three of the largest apple orchards in the valley."

Henderson studied the location on her phone. "How far away from Twin Oaks is the pay phone?"

"About ten miles." She swiped out of the app. "Sabina said the booth has been there for years, installed at the request of the orchard owners for the migrant workers to use. Cell service out there can be spotty, so having a wired phone for emergencies has come in handy."

His shoulders slumped. "No chance of surveillance cameras or usable fingerprints."

"I know you were hoping the number would lead us to Helena or, at least, to someone who could tell us who made that call."

He met her gaze, the resolve to keep looking hovering in their depths. "I was. I still think it's worth a shot to check out the booth itself."

"I'm game." Elle stuffed her notebook back into her purse and slid out of the booth. "Let's go. I'm parked right outside."

Henderson opened her car door and closed it once she was in the driver's seat. Elle punched the ignition button. It had been a long time since a man had treated her with such courtesy. A woman could get used to that.

The drive to the phone booth took less than ten minutes. Outside of town, the landscape morphed into farmland with rows of dying corn stalks and livestock. A few miles from the pay phone, apple trees, branches heavy with ripening fruit, lined the road on the left while a cornfield dominated the right-hand side.

"It should be just up ahead." She checked her mirrors. No vehicles behind her, so she slowed from the fifty-five mile per hour speed limit as they approached the intersection. The red rectangle situated on a slab of concrete appeared incongruous nestled close to fruit trees, like someone had dropped it from the sky. She pulled onto the verge and killed the engine. "Shall we?"

"Sit tight." Henderson reached for his door handle and exited the vehicle before she could respond. Rounding the hood of the car, he opened her door, holding out his hand as if she needed assistance.

Even though she didn't require help, she took the proffered hand anyway, his warm grasp sending a tingle up her arm. "Thank you."

He grinned, shedding the mantle of worry she had imagined he'd carried on the drive. The tingles expanded throughout her body at his dazzling smile.

"My mother was a stickler for what she called the 'little courtesies.'" His eyes clouded briefly. "I hope you don't mind."

"Not at all," she hastened to assure him. "You're restoring my faith in men."

His eyebrows shot up nearly to his hairline. "Then you must be hanging around the wrong kind of men."

She turned toward the phone booth to avoid allowing him to see the weight of that truth on her face.

The once fire-engine-red booth had seen better days. The overall structure appeared sound enough, but rust dotted the metal frame, and the accordion door had long since been removed. Peering inside, dust swirled around the small space and Elle sneezed.

"Bless you."

"Thanks." She continued her examination. A small shelf that had probably once held the ubiquitous phone book now gathered bits of leaves and dirt. The phone itself was marginally clean, evidence of some use on its dust-free handset. She snapped a few photos then stepped back to allow Henderson to take a look.

"Nothing much here that I can see," she said, moving to the side of the concrete slab as he took her place in front of the opening.

His entire body stiffened.

"What is it?" A shiver of unease raced down her spine.

He pointed at the shelf. "She's been here."

Elle pushed in beside him, ducking under his outstretched arm to see what had grabbed his attention. At the back of the shelf, a bundle of twigs rested. She tilted her head to see his face, the paleness kicking her heartbeat up another notch. "Why do you think Helena's been here?"

Without answering, he stepped into the booth and plucked out the twigs. Moving back out of the booth, he balanced the wood on his palm. Now that it was in the bright sunlight, she noted the twigs weren't jumbled together—they had been carefully positioned to form a tiny deer. Bits of leaf stem held the structure together.

She jerked her head up to meet Henderson's gaze. "Did—" She swallowed hard, unable to complete the question.

"My sister made these all the time when we were children." Staring at the figure in his hand, Henderson stated the obvious conclusion. "Helena is alive and near Twin Oaks."

Henderson set the deer made of twigs on top of the shelf and flexed his trembling hands. After all these years of hoping and praying and searching, here at least was tangible evidence Helena was alive. Now the sheriff would have to officially open a missing persons case.

With his phone, he snapped several photos of the deer. "I need to call my mom. Then we can tell the sheriff's office and get a forensics team out here to dust the phone for prints. If Helena made that call—and I believe she did—then her prints will be on the phone."

"Henderson."

The warning in her tone doused his excitement as thoroughly as cold water on his head.

"This isn't enough—"

"Elle, don't say it." Tears brimmed. He swallowed the emotion to regain his composure. "You have no idea what it's been like clinging to hope that Helena's alive. The uncertainty of what happened to her contributed to my dad's death, and is slowly killing my mom. I'm asking you not to spoil this moment when we finally have definitive proof she's alive. My mother and I need this moment."

"I know." Compassion flooded her expression as she laid a hand on his arm. "Call your mom, but don't call the sheriff. Not until we have hard evidence your sister did make that call."

He nodded then texted the photo of the deer to his mom, following it up with a phone call. "Mom? Did you see the photo I just sent?"

"Just a minute. I'll check." Kathleen sounded weary.

His heart ached at how difficult the last few hours must have been for her. He pivoted away from the phone booth. At the car, Elle was rummaging in the trunk.

"My daughter made that deer." The hope in her voice nearly broke him. "Did you find your sister?"

Quickly, he recounted what had happened. "We're at the phone booth now, but since it's in the middle of nowhere, there are no witnesses we can ask about who used the phone last night."

"But you're certain Helena made the deer?"

Henderson picked up the figure, the simple beauty of the creature bringing to mind lying in the clover playing Bambi with an entire herd of stick deer crafted by his sister. "As certain as I can be without firm proof."

"What does the sheriff say?"

He explained why they wouldn't be calling the sheriff. "We're making progress, Mom. Keep praying."

Elle slammed the trunk closed and returned to the booth, a plastic grocery bag in her hand.

"I've never stopped." Kathleen blew her nose. "Last night, I went through our photo albums."

The grief in her voice held a familiar ring. "Oh, Mom."

"I know I probably shouldn't have, but somehow it makes me feel closer to her."

He leaned his shoulder against the booth, images of his childhood with Helena flitting through his mind like a slide show.

"You two had such adventures together."

"That we did."

"I keep hoping that this will all turn out to be another one of her fanciful journeys." She paused before adding, "I wish there was something I could do to help search for her."

Henderson blinked back more tears. He hadn't realized how left out his mom felt—he'd only focused on her grief over his father's death and missing Helena. "Praying for her and for us as we keep looking is more important than you'll ever know."

Kathleen sniffled. "I'll not stop until she's safe back home. Please be careful, son. I love you."

"I love you too. I'll call as soon as I have more news."

Elle unpacked a pair of surgical gloves, talcum powder and a small poufy brush from a grocery bag before setting the bag on the ground. "How's she doing?"

"Hopeful." He eyed the items. "What are you going to do with those?"

She grinned. "Hopefully, pull some prints off the receiver."

"Fingerprints?"

"That's the plan." Snapping on the gloves, she uncapped the powder then dipped in the brush. "Hold this for me?" She handed him the open container.

Elle dusted the receiver lightly with the brush.

"It's not perfect, but since we know the sheriff's office won't want to waste resources sending a lab tech out here on what they would deem a fool's errand, I figured we could give it a try."

To his amazement, the powder raised several swirls that formed what appeared to his untrained eye to be fingerprints. "Wow. How'd you learn to do that?"

"YouTube." She flashed him another smile then finished coating the receiver with a light layer of powder. "I think we might be in business."

He watched in silence as she used clear tape to lift nearly a dozen prints from the receiver, transferring them to a piece of white copy paper. "Mostly partials, but—" she pointed to one that looked the most like a fingerprint "—this one is pretty much complete."

"What will you do with them? You don't have access to any law enforcement databases, so how will you get a match?" While impressed with her ingenuity, Henderson couldn't see how fingerprints without the support of the police department would be useful to finding his sister.

"I don't need to send it through a database." She slid the paper into a gallon zip-top bag and added it to the grocery bag with the rest of her makeshift fingerprint kit. "All we need to do is match one of these prints to Helena's fingerprints, assuming you have those on file."

Understanding dawned. "Actually, we do, because of her arrests. She was never charged, but she was booked once." Helena had been twenty-two and apparently desperate for a fix of whatever her then-current drug of choice. Lacking money, she had propositioned an undercover vice cop in Niagara Falls, just far enough away from Buffalo that his father hadn't heard of the arrest until after her booking.

"If you can get a copy of her prints, I know a lab tech who can compare them to see if we have a match."

"If we prove Helena did use the phone, the sheriff's office will have to open an investigation." Elation lifted some of the tension from his shoulders.

Elle didn't look quite as happy. "It's still a long shot that one of the prints will match Helena's."

"But there's also the deer." He pointed to the figurine on the phone booth shelf.

"That's circumstantial evidence. A fingerprint match would confirm Helena made the phone call, but…" she hesitated.

"But what?" The compassion in her eyes told him he didn't want to hear her fill in the blank, but the lawyer in him had asked anyway.

"It's probably not enough to have the sheriff open a missing persons case on your sister."

"Why not?" He braced himself for the answer when all his heart wanted to cling to was this slim connection to Helena.

"If we do prove Helena made that phone call to your mom, the sheriff will simply conclude she's not missing—she just doesn't want to come home."

He sighed, knowing she was right. But the truth hurt. "And therefore as an adult can't be deemed missing."

"I'm sorry. I know that's not what you want to hear. But if we do confirm Helena was here, then we should be able to find her on our own."

"I guess so." Disappointment flared. He'd pinned his hopes on finding a clue that would lead him to his sister, not raise more questions.

"Ready?" Elle turned toward the car.

"Let me get the deer." Henderson reached into the booth for the object but inadvertently knocked it to the floor as the glass at the side of the booth shattered. "Get down! Someone's shooting at us!"

SEVEN

The crack of a shot sent Elle flat on the ground to the right of the phone booth's concrete pad, her hands over her head. Glass rained down on her as another shot took out more panes. "Henderson!"

"I'm okay," he called from his position in front of the booth. He slithered off the concrete and onto the dirt as more bullets decimated the remaining glass in the booth. "Someone's shooting at us."

"Maybe we should make a run for the car?" She raised her head in time to see the windshield explode. "Or maybe not."

"I think the shooter is diagonally across the road in that orchard." He pointed in that direction as another bullet thunked into the car. Swiveling his head, he nodded toward the rows of dry corn stalks. "We might be able to lose him in the field behind us and hope he doesn't follow."

The car sank down on one side as the shooter took out a tire. Another pop convinced her the field offered a better chance of survival than staying where they were. "Okay." She drew in a deep breath and immediately regretted it as dust settled in her throat.

"On the count of three, we'll make a run for it." Henderson's calm voice gave her the strength to gather her feet underneath her as a bullet pinged off the booth frame and hit the ground inches from her body. "One. Two. Three!"

She rose to a crouch and dashed into the cornfield, the grocery bag clutched in her hand. The bag snagged on a stalk, ripping it from her hand. She turned to grab it but a shot took off the top of the stalk to the right of her head and she sprinted, leaving the bag behind. Drying stalks of corn slapped her face as she ran hunched over farther into the field. Behind her, Henderson thrashed through the corn. Soon, she only heard the cicadas buzzing and her own heavy breathing. A stitch in her side made her stumble to a halt. "Henderson?"

The stalks to her right swayed, pumping more adrenaline through her body until Henderson poked his head through, his face flushed and sweaty. "I think we're safe now," he said in a low voice as he dropped into a crouch.

She swatted a bug away from her head. "Someone was definitely shooting at us."

"But why?" Henderson wiped his forehead and neck with his sleeve.

"Because we're getting close to finding Helena?" she whispered back as they huddled together.

"Maybe." His voice held a note of confusion. "That explanation has a certain logic to it, but it doesn't make sense. There's never been any evidence Helena was kidnapped—she simply stopped contacting us nine years ago."

Elle sifted through the background material she'd read on the case. "Given her history with drugs, that must have worried you."

He nodded, his body tense as a warm breeze ruffled the tops of the dry stalks. "To be honest, there have been times when I thought she might have died." He grimaced. "Don't tell my mom, but over the years, I've visited a lot of morgues."

Her heart contracted in sympathy. "To see if an unidentified female matching Helena's basic description was your sister?"

"Yeah. Each time, it was like losing her all over again. Part of me wanted the dead woman to be Helena, to put an end to my parents' anxiety and fear." The pain in his brown eyes made her reach out and lightly touch his shoulder. "Does that make me a terrible person?"

"Not at all." Working on the podcast, she'd

seen firsthand the devastation of not knowing where a loved one was.

He rose slightly, his head nearly level with the tops of the broken stalks. Sinking back down, he spoke even softer. "At least knowing she was truly gone would give some closure and allow us to grieve. This no-man's-land of uncertainty and hope is killing my mom."

"What about you?" Elle shifted closer to him, as if her proximity would encourage confidences.

"I—" He cocked his head to one side. Finger to his lips, he motioned for her to duck even further down among the corn stalks.

She dropped lower as silently as she could, stifling the urge to cough as she inhaled dust from the dry ground. Henderson placed a hand on her forearm as the sound of someone moving slowly through the rows behind them sent her heart rate into overdrive.

Please God, don't let the shooter find us.

"They must've exited by the side road and circled back to their car," a male voice to Elle's left bellowed.

Henderson squeezed gently, reminding her to keep as still as possible. She put a hand over her mouth to stave off the desire to cough.

"Fat lot a good that will do them," another male voice chortled, "since you shot out all four tires and the windshield."

Henderson pointed to her left and slightly behind them as the source of the shooters. She nodded to show she understood where the danger was. Her body coiled in preparation of another mad dash if the perpetrators discovered their hiding place.

"Serves them Yankees right," the first man replied, a hard edge to his voice that raised the hairs on Elle's neck. "This ought a send them back up north where they belong."

Through the corn stalks, Elle caught a glimpse of one of the men, his back to her. He carried a rifle with a scope. A snake tattoo twined around his bare forearm, its mouth open and fangs bared.

The theme song to *The Dukes of Hazzard* trilled, splitting the air and making her jump. The tattooed man balanced the rifle over one elbow before tugging a phone from his back pocket.

"Looks like they've skedaddled on outta here," he said into the phone. After a short pause, he replaced the phone in his pocket then called to his companion. "Someone alerted the sheriff's office about the vehicle. Boss wants us back at the compound pronto. Let's go."

As the two men noisily walked away through the cornfield, she rocked back on her heels, letting her butt hit the ground as the adrenaline drained from her body. Her mind swirled with what they'd overheard but laser focused on one phrase: the compound.

She would have to redouble her efforts to figure out what that meant and what, if any, was its connection to Helena Parker.

Henderson checked his watch. Ten minutes had passed since the two men had left the cornfield. In the distance, a siren whopped. Beside him, Elle sat on the ground between the rows, her face flushed and her hair mussed, but no tears. Instead, the upward tilt to her chin told him the shooting had firmed her resolve to find Helena rather than scare her off the trail. He'd met many calm, competent women as an assistant DA, but those were usually attorneys or in law enforcement, which made Elle's response to the shooting all the more admirable. She hadn't lost her head or started crying—either of which would have been understandable in the circumstances.

"I hear sirens," she said. "Do you think it's safe to get out of the field?"

He listened as the sound of help arriving grew louder. "Yeah." Standing, he held out his hand to help her to her feet. "Are you okay?"

She brushed her backside, sending dirt and debris to the ground. "I think so. Man, am I thirsty. I hope they didn't shoot up the cooler in the trunk."

At the mention of a cooler, he became aware of how dry his mouth was. "With water?"

"Yes. I always try to have some snacks and water on hand because I never know where tracking down sources will take me."

"Let's go." He took her hand, grateful for her resourcefulness.

She followed him through the stalks. "I hope you know where you're headed, as I can't see above the stalks."

His six-foot-one frame nearly cleared the corn, giving him enough of a view that he could discern the direction of the road. "It's this way."

Flashing blue and red lights helped identify the correct path. Soon, they stepped from the field. Two sheriff cruisers were parked on the shoulder near Elle's car. One deputy circled her vehicle, snapping photos with a digital camera, while the other deputy squatted by the phone booth.

At their approach, the closer deputy rose, his hand moving to the butt of his gun, then recognition settled on his face and his posture relaxed. "Mr. Parker, Ms. Updike, are you okay?"

"I think so, Deputy Stubbs," Henderson said.

"What happened?" Stubbs asked.

"Two men started shooting at us while we were standing by the phone booth," Henderson said.

"They sure did a number on your car," the other deputy chimed in before introducing himself as Wayne Driscoll. "All four tires and the windshield."

Elle hurried over, key fob in hand. "I hope the trunk release still works." She hit the button and the trunk lid popped open. "Thank goodness the cooler's intact."

Henderson answered the questioning look on Stubbs' face. "We're thirsty."

Elle returned with two water bottles, offering one to Henderson before cracking open her own and taking a long swallow. "There's more if you and the other deputy want one."

"We're good, thanks," Stubbs said. He stepped back to use his lapel mic to relay something to Dispatch, but Henderson couldn't decipher what the coded numbers meant. When he finished, he turned his attention back to Henderson and Elle.

"You want to walk me through what happened?" The deputy glanced around him. "Looks like someone was determined to hit all the glass in the booth and disable your car."

Henderson succinctly relayed the shooting, not saying why they happened to be at the phone booth, with Elle interjecting facts along the way. Throughout his recitation, Stubbs asked a few clarifying questions, but with his eyes hidden behind aviator sunglasses, Henderson couldn't tell what the man was thinking.

"So what brought you two out here to begin with?"

Henderson exchanged a glance with Elle, who

shrugged as if to say it was his call. Surely, with the shooting, knowing Helena called Kathleen from this phone booth would be enough to push the sheriff's office into investigating her disappearance. "Last night, my mom received a phone call from my sister."

Stubbs looked up from his notebook. "The one you said is missing?"

Henderson didn't miss the note of disbelief in the deputy's voice. Missing people didn't call their mothers. "Yes, Helena Parker."

"What did she say?"

Henderson recounted the brief conversation. "My mom's caller ID had this phone number on it."

"The phone booth number?" Stubbs tapped the pen on his notebook.

"Yes, so Elle and I drove out to take a look." Henderson drained the water bottle.

"What did you find?"

"A little deer figurine…" Henderson didn't finish his thought as he suddenly remembered reaching for the deer on the shelf when the bullets started flying. He stepped around the deputy and peered into the booth. No deer sat on the shelf, no bits of wood lay anywhere. "It's gone."

"Oh, no," Elle said. "Maybe it got knocked out. I'll look on the back side."

"Hold on, this is crime scene, so no unauthorized snooping allowed." Stubbs' voice brooked no arguments. "Describe this deer, and we'll have the crime scene tech do a thorough search when documenting the scene."

Henderson gave a description as he pulled out his phone. "Here, I took several photos." He showed the deputy then sent him the photos at Stubbs's request. "It's an exact replica of ones my sister used to make when we were kids."

"I see." Stubbs didn't seem as convinced as Henderson that the deer was a clue Helena had called their mom from the phone booth.

"Elle lifted fingerprints from the receiver," Henderson added.

"I did, but I lost the bag when we entered the cornfield. I was going to look once we've given the deputy our statements, but I'm not sure I can find it again."

Driscoll approached. "I called a tow truck, and it should be here within the hour to take your car to our crime scene lab to recover the bullets, then we'll send it over to Dave's Auto Body on the outskirts of Twin Oaks."

"Thank you." Elle's shoulders drooped. "I'd better inform the insurance company what happened. When will I be able to get a copy of your report?"

"We'll need you both to come down to the office sometime tomorrow to sign your statements, and the admin can make a copy of our report for you then," Stubbs said.

"Will you open an investigation into my sister's disappearance?" Henderson couldn't keep the hope from his voice.

Stubbs shook his head. "By your account, she's not missing since you believe she called your mom yesterday. It sounds like she just doesn't want to come home."

Henderson wanted to shake the man for not seeing the forest for the trees. Elle laid a hand on his arm, her light touch reminding him he wasn't in this alone. She smiled at the deputy. "Do you have any idea as to who shot at us and why?"

"We'll do our best, but your description is pretty vague."

"Except for the tattoo," she said.

"Even that isn't as unusual as you seem to think. Lots of people have tattoos." Stubbs held up a hand. "But I plan to check with our gang expert to see if any local groups use snakes. As to the why, we do get random shootings of old buildings. Perhaps someone was taking potshots at the phone booth."

"And we got in the way?" Henderson had worked with cops like Stubbs, who had little imagination at all when it came to solving crimes. "We're strangers in town. The only reason we're both here is to find Helena. My room has been searched, someone left a poisonous snake in Elle's room, and now we've been shot at by two men who said they were deliberately trying to get us to leave town."

Stubbs shook his head again. "Now, hold on. We can't connect the break-in with this shooting. As for the snake, sometimes they enter homes all on their own."

"I don't believe this." Henderson's chest tightened as anger coursed through his veins. "That copperhead didn't just slither up the stairs and into Elle's bathroom. You can't be stupid enough to believe that."

Stubbs snapped his notebook closed and pocketed it, along with his ballpoint pen. "I think we're done here. Our crime scene unit is on its way to collect evidence from the scene. Come by the station tomorrow to sign your statements. Driscoll will wait here for the techs to arrive."

Henderson started to say something but Elle tugged on his arm. He glanced down at her and she shook her head, her eyes warning him to let it go.

Driscoll touched the brim of his hat briefly before climbing into his cruiser as Stubbs drove off.

Henderson paced toward the road to avoid the glass littering the ground around the booth. "Can you believe him? How could he not see that these incidents have to be connected with our looking for Helena? Why is he being so obtuse?"

"Obtuse?" Elle's voice held a note of levity. "That's a fifty-cent word, as my grandmother used to say."

Henderson whirled to glare at her. "What has that to do with anything?"

"Sorry, my attempt at a little humor."

He folded his arms across his chest at her poor timing coupled with the lack of cooperation from law enforcement. "Maybe I should take this directly to the sheriff. There has to be a way to convince him to open an investigation."

"Would the *evidence* we have so far convince you?"

He narrowed his eyes. "What's that supposed to mean?"

"You're an assistant district attorney. If someone brought you this case as it stands—not your suppositions and instinct as a brother—but the bare facts, would it be enough for the police to pursue?"

Her words rang true, but he was too angry to heed sound counsel. "I thought you understood what I was trying to do."

She held up her hands in mock surrender. "I'm on your side, remember? But I think you're too close to the situation and need to step back to gain perspective."

"That's rich, coming from someone who preys on the grief and drama of others for a living." The color drained from her face, but that didn't stop the flow of words. "I shouldn't have trusted a journalist."

Elle opened her mouth but snapped it closed. She turned away from him though not before he registered a shimmer of tears in her eyes.

How had he let his frustration and fear boil over to the point where he hurt the woman trying to help him? "Elle, I—"

Elle headed toward the side of the road, leaving him to wonder if his best chance of following this slim lead to his sister had just walked away.

EIGHT

Nestled in the comfy armchair in her room, Elle breathed deeply the scents of the eucalyptus-and-tea essential oil blend she'd dabbed on her pulse points. Her run through the cornfield had left its mark in the form of dozens of small scratches, most of which hadn't drawn blood but still stung. She sipped sparkling water and tried to forget the tense ride back to town in the back of Driscoll's car. The deputy had dropped her off at Dave's Auto Body so she could discuss her car with him.

True to Driscoll's word, Dave Tremaine, owner of Dave's Auto Body, had been willing to take charge of her vehicle once the technicians had finished their investigation. He'd even offered to discuss the damage and potential repairs with her insurance company. While Henderson stalked off, presumably to head back to Tall Trees B and B, Elle had connected Dave with her insurance rep, then grabbed takeout from the diner to take to her room.

Now, she popped a fry into her mouth while contemplating her next move. First, she'd get Sabina to research compounds in Shenandoah County. Elle's initial Google search had turned up zilch, but Sabina had a way of flushing out obscure information. Second, she'd update Caren on the status of the investigation and figure out how to work the day's events into an episode.

Pulling her laptop toward her, she booted up, zipped through her email and then sent Sabina a detailed note about the additional research needed. Her phone trilled just as she hit Send on her email to Sabina. Her pulse raced even though her head told her it wouldn't be Henderson calling. Caller ID showed it was her editor.

"Hi, Caren," Elle said. "You will not believe what happened today."

"Did it involve the hunky assistant DA?"

Elle grimaced at the hint of expectation in Caren's voice. "Mr. Parker was with me."

"Then I'm all ears."

Elle recounted the day's events, ending with Henderson's declaration that he shouldn't trust journalists.

"You're not going to take him seriously, are you?"

"If by that you mean am I going to stop working with him on finding his sister? The answer is no." Elle pinched the bridge of her nose as the headache that had been threatening all day suddenly decided to make its presence known.

"That's not all I meant," Caren said. "I do care about you more than the show."

"I know you do." Elle fumbled for her bag to extract a few aspirin tablets. "But since that's all there is between Henderson Parker and myself..." She didn't finish the thought. Instead, she downed the aspirin with a sip of water. If only she could wash away the hurt from Henderson's words.

"Girl, don't try to tell me you don't care a teeny, tiny bit about what Mr. Tall, Dark, and Handsome thinks about you as a woman—and that he's beginning to get under your skin in a decidedly nonprofessional way."

"He's a source." She needed to get Caren off this topic and fast before Elle revealed just how attractive she found Henderson. The way he'd tried to protect her from the shooters made her go all gooey inside, like the perfect brownie middle. And don't get her started about the way the man listened, his intense brown eyes conveying that whatever she was saying was the most important thing in the world to him. But he'd made it very clear his top priority was finding his sister, much like the men who expressed interest in her only to want to meet her father. She would do well to remember that and avoid getting hurt again. "Did you listen to yesterday's interview?"

"I know what you're doing. If I weren't your

producer as well as your friend, I wouldn't let you get away with it," Caren warned. "Your interview with Parker was good. I'm already working on how to chop it up into several episodes. Here's what I'm thinking."

For the next hour, Elle and Caren hashed out the first episode of *Gone Without a Trace*. But when Elle said goodbye to Caren and set her phone alarm for 7:00 a.m., it wasn't the podcast that filled her thoughts. Instead, her mind focused on whether or not Henderson's beard was soft or scratchy to the touch—and if she'd ever be close enough to find out. With a shake of her head, she dashed those thoughts to the ground. She wouldn't let herself be caught up in romantic what-ifs. If she kept to the script, she might make it through with her heart intact.

Henderson tossed back the covers and swung his legs over the side of the bed. Two fifteen. Maybe some warm milk might settle his thoughts. Shoving his feet into slides, he stretched as he took a quick inventory of his pajamas. An old T-shirt and cotton shorts made him presentable enough if he happened to run into anyone.

Alec and Isabella had insisted their guests could raid the fridge for a snack anytime day or night. Henderson hoped he wouldn't wake anyone during his forage trip. He snagged his phone and left his room.

In the hallway, he stared at Elle's closed door, no sliver of light peeking underneath the solid oak. Fast asleep, like he should be. And he likely would have been had he not chickened out and put off apologizing to Elle for calling her an unscrupulous journalist. His lame excuse to himself that he was upset about the lack of interest from law enforcement didn't cut the mustard, as his grandfather used to say.

Shaking his head, Henderson continued to the kitchen. He poured milk into a pan then heated it slowly on the large gas stove. After transferring the warm milk into a mug, he washed the pan.

"Couldn't sleep?"

Henderson tensed, dish towel in hand, at the sound of a man's voice. Then Alec Stratman came into the light.

"No. My mom always made warm milk to help us sleep, and I thought it might do the trick tonight." Henderson replaced the dish towel on the fridge handle.

"My aunt swore by the same remedy."

The two men shared a smile. Henderson picked up his mug. "I hope I didn't wake you."

Alec waved his hand. "My wife swears I can detect any 'disturbance' in the house atmosphere, so here I am." He shrugged. "Not sure that's always a good thing, but it kept me alive through three tours in Iraq and Afghanistan."

Henderson sipped the milk, the warm liquid

soothing his tangled thoughts. "You were in the army, right?"

As Alec made his own warm milk, he shared a little about his military service and how he and Isabella had come to own this house, which had been his great-aunt's. "We opened for our first guests about a year ago."

Leaning against the counter, Henderson drank more milk while Alec washed the pan. Then the former army captain picked up his own mug. "Enough about me. Something's gotten you up at this hour."

Henderson appreciated the other man's indirect opening for him to share. Instinct urged him to trust Alec. "You know I'm in town looking for my sister, who vanished going on nine years ago."

Alec nodded. "I saw a couple of your posters around town and Isabella said something about a photo from the Twin Oaks Christmas in July parade?"

Henderson outlined everything that had happened, sticking to the bare facts. When he'd finished both the story and his milk, he rinsed his mug and loaded it into the dishwasher. Then he voiced a question that had been bothering him. "What do you know about Deputy Stubbs?"

Alec added his cup to the top rack before closing the dishwasher. "Deputy Stubbs joined the sheriff's office about eight months ago, and I've only encountered him a handful of times." He gazed out the window above the sink into the inky blackness beyond, his features slightly blurry in the reflection.

Henderson waited, sensing the other man had something more to add.

"In my army stint, I met all kinds of men and women, and I learned to judge a person rather quickly." Alec turned to face Henderson. "I've never heard anything negative about Stubbs from town gossip."

"But…" Henderson prompted, sensing there was more to come.

"But my gut tells me he's hiding something."

Henderson had been expecting that answer, yet it still punched him in the midsection. "Are you saying we shouldn't count on Stubbs to be an ally in our search for my sister?"

"I wouldn't go that far, but I would say to be very careful in your dealings with him until you find out more." Alec yawned. "It's probably a good thing another deputy came to the scene yesterday."

Henderson immediately caught the implication. "Therefore, Stubbs has to write an accurate report about the incident."

"You're catching on," Alec said. "Although, as a prosecutor, the possibility of someone in law enforcement out for themselves shouldn't come as a surprise to you."

"It doesn't," he agreed. "Elle basically told me

the same thing today—that I haven't been looking at this case with my assistant district attorney hat on. If I had been, I would have seen the
thinness of the evidence and understood the re-
luctance of the sheriff's office to open a missing
persons case for Helena."

Alec smothered another yawn. "You didn't listen to her, did you?"

"No," he admitted. "Instead, I called her a
muckraking journalist."

Alec raised his eyebrows. "Ouch, that must
have ruffled her feathers."

"You have no idea." Again, Henderson silently
berated himself for not attempting to apologize
to her.

"My advice? Grovel when you apologize.
Good night."

Henderson followed the man out of the kitchen,
mulling the excellent advice. As he climbed the
stairs to his room, an idea bloomed in his mind on
how he could convince Elle how very sorry he was.

The scent of bacon teased her nostrils as Elle
exited her room. Henderson's door was closed as
she passed on her way to the stairs. Maybe she'd
run into him in the dining room. Relief mingled
with disappointment at the sight of Isabella tidy-
ing the room but no Henderson.

Isabella greeted her as she entered the dining
room. "Good morning, Elle. It's going to be an-

other hot one today. But you're dressed for the heat, I see."

Elle glanced down at her sunshine-yellow sleeveless knit dress and strappy sandals. "Seemed the most sensible thing to wear."

"It's adorable on you." Isabella poured her coffee. "I've set up breakfast on the sideboard today, as we're hosting the Rotary breakfast in half an hour."

"Oh, I forgot about that. I'll eat fast." Elle headed to the buffet and picked up a plate. Behind her, Isabella restocked condiments on the individual tables. Selecting fluffy scrambled eggs and a few pieces of bacon, she returned to her seat after scanning the room for signs Henderson had been down before her.

"If you're wondering, Henderson had his breakfast an hour ago."

A blush heated her cheeks. "What he does is none of my business."

Isabelle chuckled. "Which is why the man's eyes barely strayed from the dining room doorway the entire time he ate."

Elle mulled that over as she enjoyed the crisp bacon and eggs, her heart beating a little faster as she considered the reasons. He could have either wanted to avoid her or wanted to see her. She had no way of knowing which one it was, since she had taken her time getting ready for the day. Better to focus on the tasks ahead of her. "Isabella?"

The other woman stopped by her table, her arms full of dark green napkins, reminding Elle of the upcoming business breakfast.

"Never mind. You're busy. It can wait."

Isabella dropped into the opposite chair, laying the napkins on the table. "I can fold the napkins here as well as at another table, so go ahead. What's on your mind?"

"I overheard one of the men yesterday say something about a compound. My researcher couldn't find any references to such a place in the area." Sabina's report had been a major disappointment, as the researcher had only discovered farms, none of which were ever called or alluded to as a compound.

"Compound? Like where hippies live in communal bliss?"

"I guess so. I actually have no idea." Elle finished her breakfast. "All I know is that's where the shooters were headed."

Isabella continued to transform the napkins into elaborate triangles, her forehead wrinkled. "Let's see... There's Appleby's Orchards, Koon's Orchards, Daisy's Farm, Triple Z Farm, and Homer's Honey. I think that's all the farms and orchards within a twenty-five-mile radius to Twin Oaks."

"Which are the closest to the phone booth?"

"That would be Koon's and Daisy's. Daisy's butts right up against the booth. You were in their cornfields." She finished the last napkin and stood. "I'll ask Alec, as he might have heard one of those referred to as a compound, although I doubt it. All of them have been operating for generations."

Disappointment filled Elle's belly, along with the eggs, bacon and coffee. "Thanks." She rose as well, stacking her plate, silverware and empty cup. "I'll take these through to the kitchen."

Isabella reached for the plate. "You don't have to do that."

Elle twisted her body to keep the items out of Isabella's reach. "You have enough on your plate right now."

"Bad pun," the other woman retorted, "but considering I have ten minutes before the Rotary Club members come, I'll let you do it. But just for today."

"Yes, ma'am." Elle winked then scurried off to the kitchen, where she found Alec washing dishes. "Here are a few more for you."

"Thanks." He didn't comment on why Elle had brought in her own dishes.

"Your wife was listing all the farms and orchards in the area, but said none of them were known as a compound. Have you ever heard that term in connection with a specific location around here?"

"Compound? Nope." He scrubbed a skillet vigorously before rinsing it. "Which ones did she mention?"

Elle recounted the list, which she had jotted down in her notes app for future reference.

"She did forget one."

Her antenna pricked up. "Oh? Which one was that?"

Alec paused, his soapy hands dangling over the edge of the sink. "It's fairly new, compared to the other farms. Someone bought the old Dermott place about eight or ten years ago—I can't remember exactly."

"Was it a large piece of property?"

"I think around three hundred acres. Old man Dermott's will stipulated his kids couldn't sell it to a developer, so it took them a few years to find a buyer for the entire spread."

"Where is it located?"

Alec finished the pan and set it in the drainer. Dish towel in hand, he turned to her. "The property line is less than two miles from the phone booth."

Elle tapped in the information into her notes app. "Could you spell Dermott?"

Alec did. "You seem excited about this information."

"It's probably nothing, but I'll check out the property records to see who bought the place then drive out to see it for myself." Elle thanked him and returned to her room to send Sabina a quick email asking her to dig into who bought the Dermott farm right away. Elle could grab another cup of coffee at The Beanery while she waited for Sabina to check online property records. Plan in hand, she hustled out the front door, sidestepping a steady stream of men and women in business attire entering the bed-and-breakfast. Presumably the Rotary Club members.

On the pathway, she paused to one side to put on her sunglasses. When she turned to continue her journey, Henderson blocked her path, a bouquet of wildflowers in his hands. Her resolve to focus only on finding his missing sister weakened at the anxious expression in his brown eyes, but she waited to see if he would add a verbal apology to the beautiful bouquet. Breathing in the sweet aroma of fresh-cut flowers, she schooled her face to give nothing away and told her fluttering heart to stop wishing for things that couldn't be. No matter how much she didn't want it to be true, Henderson was likely only bringing her flowers because he needed her help.

NINE

Henderson clutched the blossoms as a shield. No apology had seemed quite as difficult as this one, maybe because there was so much riding since he needed Elle's help. Ignoring the little voice whispering that it wasn't the only reason for his attack of the nerves, he drew in a deep breath. "Elle."

"Mr. Parker." She acknowledged him, her eyes frosty in the warm sunlight.

Her formal greeting wasn't a good sign. She moved past him.

"Wait, please." His words halted her progress, but she didn't turn around. A few men hurried past him, throwing him curious glances. He didn't want an audience, but he also couldn't let her leave without telling her how wrong he had been. "I'm sorry."

Squaring his shoulders, he rounded in front of her. "I said terrible things about you and your work. I was frustrated with the deputy's response, but that's no excuse to take it out on you." He thrust the flowers at her. "Please accept these and my sincere apology."

For one awful moment, she didn't move. Then her hands reached for the bouquet. "These are lovely."

His shoulders relaxed a fraction. So far, so good. "I'm truly very sorry."

She buried her face in the flowers. "When you put it that way, I forgive you."

"Thank you." A smile stretched his face. Why her accepting his apology should make him feel so happy, he didn't want to examine right now. "And I would be happy to drive you to the sheriff's office to sign our statements."

Her brow furrowed. "Oh, right. I'd forgotten we need to do that. Let me put these in water and we can go." She darted up the porch stairs.

A few minutes later, they were headed toward the sheriff's office in Woodstock, Virginia, half an hour away.

The office bustled with activity—people coming and going in a steady stream. Henderson expected they would have to wait, but a different deputy came out right away with their statements on clipboards. After reviewing and signing the paperwork, the deputy thanked them but could give no updates on the shooting or break-in.

Back in the SUV, Henderson punched on the ignition and blasted the AC. "Where to next?"

"The old Dermott farm. Sabina—that's *Gone*'s

researcher—found an address." She entered it into a map app, which began giving directions as Henderson put the shift in gear.

"Why are we going there?" He pulled out of the parking lot.

Elle told him about her conversation with Alec. "It's the only large piece of property no one seems to know much about. I know it's a long shot, but I thought it would be worth checking out." Her phone pinged with a text from Sabina.

Henderson drove for a few minutes while Elle studied her phone.

"Sabina found some information about the property. A corporation called Manifestum Holdings bought the farm from the Dermott estate nine years ago for $850,000."

"How big was the farm?" Henderson turned onto another state road, heading south toward Twin Oaks.

"According to the deed, it's three hundred and twelve acres, with a farmhouse, a barn, paddock, and various other outbuildings."

"And Manifestum Holdings is on the deed?"

"Yep, but it's a shell company—it has a single-page website with its name, some generic business language, and a post office box for its address." Elle sighed. "Guess who owns Manifestum?"

Henderson slowed as the route took them through the center of Twin Oaks. "Another company?"

"Bingo. This one's called Filii Dei Incorporated." She was reading from her phone. "Sabina says there are several more layers to dig through to get to an actual name, but she'll keep going."

"Not all shell companies are involved in illegal activities." He glanced out the passenger's-side window as they passed the shattered phone booth. A half a mile later, the guidance system told them to turn left onto a narrower road.

"We're getting close, another mile or so." Elle slipped on sunglasses.

The road curved to the right then the map's navigation voice informed them their destination was on the left. If he hadn't been driving slower than the posted fifty miles per hour speed limit, he would have blown right past the driveway. "Not a good sign it's in use," he said as he carefully drove his rental SUV over a cattle grate and onto a dirt road lined with overgrown bushes dripping with honeysuckle and Virginia creeper.

The vines grew so thickly, their leaves kissed the vehicle's sides as he guided the SUV carefully down the lane. About fifty feet in, the brambles gave way to trees. Soon, a gate halted their progress. Beyond the fence lay fields heavy with what appeared to be wheat to Henderson's untrained eyes. A large sign posted on the gate informed them they were on private property, warning No Trespassing.

"Another dead end." He reached for the gear-shift to put the SUV in reverse.

"Wait." Elle craned her neck, her eyes focused on the fence. "Do you see that camera?"

He followed her pointing finger to see a small camera nearly hidden on the top of the gate, its lens facing their vehicle.

"And there's one on the right and left gateposts too." She exchanged a look with him. "Awful lot of security cameras for a deserted farm."

"You think someone's watching us right now?"

"I wouldn't be surprised. Let's go before they send someone to see what we're up to."

"Too late." Henderson nodded toward a Jeep bouncing down the lane, two burly men visible through the open frame.

"Stay here unless I motion for you to join me." Before he could protest, Elle opened her door as the Jeep slid to a stop in a cloud of dust. Stepping out, she waved at the men. "Hello!"

Henderson powered down his window to follow the conversation. The passenger disembarked, walking toward the gate with a high-powered rifle in his hands. A sliver of unease tightened Henderson's hands on the steering wheel.

"This is private property," the man barked, his eyes hidden behind dark sunglasses.

Elle smiled. "Don't worry, I saw the sign. We were just figuring out where we went wrong when you came along to rescue us."

The man frowned. "You need to leave."

"And we will. We were looking for Route 639, but somehow ended up on 739." She fluttered her hands. "We're looking for the Smith place to pick up an antique mirror but lost cell reception halfway there and must have taken a wrong turn. Would you kindly point us in the right direction?"

During her speech, the driver exited the Jeep and walked over. His body language was more open and relaxed than his companion's. "What's the matter?"

"She's trespassing and needs to leave." The man slung the gun barrel upward, resting it over his shoulder. The movement pushed up the sleeve of his cuffed button-down khaki shirt, revealing some sort of tattoo, but Henderson couldn't quite make out the design.

Elle brought her hands to her chest. "Oh, I'm so sorry. We certainly did not mean to trespass. I was just explaining that we're lost."

"I see." The driver regarded her then reached into his pocket to extract a phone. He glanced at the screen.

"Yes, we were looking for—"

"I'm sorry, but we won't be able to help you," the driver's demeanor shifted from amenable to shuttered in a blink of an eye. "You need to leave now."

"Okay." She held up her hands in the universal gesture of appeasement. "Sorry to have bothered you."

"And don't come back," the driver called. "We won't respond so *kindly* to a second visit."

Elle scampered back to the SUV, sliding in and buckling her seat belt with shaking fingers. "Go!"

With no place to turn around, Henderson threw the gear into reverse and guided the vehicle back down the lane. "Are they watching us?"

"Yes." Elle's breathing hitched. "They scared me."

"Me too." Henderson hit the brakes to check for oncoming traffic before reversing onto the road. "You okay?"

"I'll feel better once we put some distance between us and them." Elle caught her breath. "But continue on the way we were headed. I'd like to see if we can tell how much of the property fronts the road."

Henderson swung out onto the road. "You're frightened but still thinking like a reporter."

"Can't help it, I guess." Her heartbeat slowed. "See those No Trespassing signs tacked to the posts among the brambles? I think that's the Dermott property line."

Checking his rearview mirror for traffic and seeing no one behind him, Henderson slowed to squint at the signs placed every fifty yards or so. "Is that barbed-wire fencing?"

"I think there is barbed wire, but I also think

it's electrified." She paused. "Did you see the tattoo on the gunman's forearm?"

"I saw something, but couldn't make it out." His stomach clenched in anticipation of her next words.

"It was a snake with fangs showing, encircling the arm with the same color scheme as the one the shooter had." The tension in her voice matched the coiling in his midsection. "But the voices weren't the same."

"What are the odds two men would have identical tattoos?"

Their eyes met briefly before Henderson returned his attention to the road.

"If it were only a snake, I'd say pretty high. But add the distinctive coloring and bared fangs, and the odds should drop dramatically." She shook her head. "I wish I'd been able to snap a photo of the tattoo—would make things much easier to trace."

"Maybe the deputy will be able to find out if it's a gang marking or not." Alec's observation about Stubbs flitted through his mind. Henderson didn't want to cast suspicion on someone, especially one in law enforcement, without solid proof the deputy wasn't doing his job, so he didn't say anything to Elle.

They came to a cross street with the optimistic name of Hope Road. "Right or left?"

"Left."

He turned onto the narrow paved lane. Along the left, more No Trespassing signs and fencing. A mile down, he spotted a bright blue mailbox on the right. "Maybe a neighbor might know something about who's living on the old Dermott place."

She grinned. "Exactly what I was going to suggest."

Turning onto the gravel drive, he drove about a mile before reaching a whitewashed, two-story farmhouse with a large, wraparound front porch. A fenced vegetable garden took over much of the right side yard, with a freestanding garage to the left of the house. A pair of dogs raced around from the back of the house, barking up a storm as Henderson cut the engine. The canines surrounded the SUV, yipping louder. Beside him, Elle trembled, fear pouring off her like water cascading over a cliff. An urge to protect her welled up inside him. He might have failed Helena, but he would not fail to keep Elle safe.

Elle shrank back in her seat, terror immobilizing her.

"Hey, you okay?"

She jumped when Henderson touched the back of her hand. "Yes. No." She squeezed her hands together but couldn't stop the shaking.

"I don't think the dogs will hurt us."

"You don't know that." Her breath hitched as

she tried to regulate her intake of air. "I don't like dogs."

A piercing whistle split the air and the animals loped away from the vehicle.

Closing her eyes, Elle scrambled to regain her composure. She was not getting out of the vehicle as long as those dogs were loose.

Henderson climbed out, shutting the door. In the quiet of the SUV's interior, she prayed for calm. A tapping on the window startled her.

Henderson bent down. "He's putting the dogs in their pen. It's safe to come out."

Her eyes strayed beyond him to see a man in overalls and a straw hat securing the latch of a run under the shade of several trees just beyond the garage.

"Okay."

He opened her door, extending a hand to help her. She nearly refused but her still wobbly legs convinced her to accept his assistance. "Thank you."

"My pleasure." He patted her shoulder as the man returned.

"Sorry about that." The man was much younger than Elle had expected, probably barely thirty. "Megs and Theo can get a little rambunctious when visitors arrive."

"Thanks for putting them up while we're here," she said. "I'm Elle Updike."

"Howard Gray." He shook her hand. "What

brings you to Hope Farm? If you're looking for eggs, we'll have some more tomorrow. A fox frightened the hens last night and the morning's take was a wee bit off."

"We're not here to buy something," Elle said. "We're actually hoping you can tell us something about your neighbor across the road."

Gray scratched the back of his neck. "I think you'd better come inside."

Elle threw Henderson a glance at the invitation, but followed the farmer up the steps and into the cool house.

"Milly? Company." Gray called out after they'd entered. "Come on back to the kitchen. It's bread-baking day, and Milly will be up to her elbows in dough."

In the cheery kitchen with white cabinets and apples stenciled on the cabinet doors, a pregnant woman a few years younger than Gray pounded dough on a long kitchen table. A fat-cheeked baby gurgled and bounced on chubby legs in a doorway jumper.

"Ms. Updike, Mr. Parker, this is my wife, Milly, and our baby, Jesse," Gray introduced. "These folks have some questions about our neighbors."

Milly flipped the dough before driving her fist into the mound again. "The co-op hippies?"

Elle's attention caught on the word choice, but she'd come back to that after introducing why they wanted to know. "I'm a podcaster with *Gone Without a Trace*, and I'm helping Mr. Parker find his missing sister." She nodded at Henderson. "Show them a photo of Helena."

He pulled up the photo on his phone and showed each Gray, but neither recognized Helena.

"Howie, why don't you fix them something to drink while I set the dough to rise," his wife said.

Gray served them ice water and settled them in the family room. Henderson peppered Gray with questions about the farm until Milly entered with her own glass.

"Baby's down for his nap. You didn't get started without me, did you?"

"Wouldn't dream of it." Her husband laughed.

Both Grays turned as one toward Elle and Henderson, who nodded at Elle to share however much she thought prudent. "Thanks for taking the time to talk with us about the 'co-op,' did you call it?"

"It's called the Sonshine Co-op." Milly set the rocking chair in motion, her hand resting on her swollen belly.

"Sunshine Co-op?" Elle pulled out her phone and opened the notes app.

"With an *o* instead of a *u*," Milly clarified. "They're a group of what used to be called hippies, running a cooperative with back-to-the-earth kind of principals."

"Like what?" Elle corrected the spelling in her notes.

"My wife is being kind," Gray said. "They're a bunch of city slickers who decided farming would be the way to create a utopia."

"You don't sound like you like them very much," Henderson observed.

"I don't." His mouth turned down at the corners. "They claim to be organic farmers, but I don't think they are."

"Now, don't be such a grump. You'll have to excuse my husband," Milly said, her eyes shining with love, "but he's had a bee in his bonnet about the co-op ever since one of their watermelons bested ours at the county fair a few weeks ago."

"It's more than just the watermelon contest," Gray protested. "At the local farmers market, they've been turning up with fruit and vegetables so shiny, you'd think they fell off a refrigerator truck, not grown on a farm."

"They certainly have no problem selling their wares." Milly's voice held a note of reproof that silenced whatever else her husband might have added.

Gray laughed but his eyes held no mirth. "My wife thinks I'm jealous because they've had a very successful season."

Elle suspected the pair had discussed this before but wisely didn't press Gray for what he hadn't said.

"And we have too," Milly interjected.

"That's right." Gray slapped his hands on his knees and rose. "And if we're to have anything for this Saturday's market, I'd best get out in the fields."

Elle also got to her feet. "Is there anything else about the co-op you haven't mentioned?"

Gray shook his head, but Milly spoke up. "Do you think we should tell them about all the vehicles we noticed when we first lived here?"

"Vehicles?" Henderson parroted.

Gray rubbed his chin. "We called the sheriff's office a lot when we first bought this place three years ago because of all the traffic going by our house. There's another access point about a half mile farther down Hope Road."

"We moved out here to get away from the traffic, and we certainly didn't want to listen to the roar of cars and trucks all night long," Milly added.

"What do you think was going on?" Elle picked up her empty glass.

"I suspected drugs, but the sheriff's office took a look then told us the neighbors were just having multiple parties. I think they were fined for operating an event without the proper permits," Gray said.

"Did the late-night traffic stop?" Henderson leaned forward.

"For the most part," Milly said. "We occasionally hear a car or two drive by but we can't say for certain where they're headed."

"Thanks," Henderson said, joining Elle with his glass in hand.

Elle hurried to ask her final question. "Have you ever seen anyone with some sort of snake tattoo with fangs?"

Milly frowned. "Yes. That man who used to come by to buy eggs for his wife, you know the one with the scraggly hair. He had one of those on his arm."

"Did he?" Gray shrugged. "I don't recall, but you're the one who dealt with the roadside customers."

Milly picked up an envelope and a pen. "Here's what it looked like." She drew for a couple of minutes and then handed Elle the envelope.

Elle stared down at the snake circling an arm, its mouth wide open and deadly fangs poised. "You're quite talented." She didn't mention it was the same tattoo she'd seen on one of the shooter's arms and peeking out from under the sleeve of the man holding the rifle on co-op property.

Milly blushed as her husband put in, "She drew the apples in the kitchen."

"I'm impressed," Elle said. "I can't draw a straight line with a ruler." She held up the envelope. "May I keep this?"

"Sure," Milly said.

"We've taken up enough of your time," Henderson said. "Thank you for the information."

"I'll walk you out," Gray said as they told Milly goodbye.

Outside, Gray lowered his voice. "I didn't want say anything in front of Milly, as she tends to fret, and that's not good for the baby, but I've been having trouble with crop theft."

Elle wrinkled her nose. "Someone's stealing your crops?"

"Not a lot, but this morning when I went to dig potatoes, one row had already been dug up. Only holes where there used to be potatoes. I always fill in the holes to even out the ground when I dig."

"What do you think is happening?" Henderson asked.

"I think someone from the co-op is taking my food. Not enough to sell, but just enough to for a small family to eat," Gray said.

"Have you informed the sheriff?" Elle said.

Gray shook his head. "And say what? They'd probably put it down to animals. No, I think it's someone who's hungry and doesn't have any other way to get food. But since there's only the co-op across the street and a few trailer homes on small parcels of land farther down the road, I thought I'd mention it."

"Thanks," Henderson said. "Appreciate it." He handed the man a card. "My number's on the back if you happen to remember anything else that might be useful."

Gray tucked the card into his overall's front pocket. "Hope you find your sister."

Back in the SUV, Elle and Henderson compared notes as they headed back to Tall Trees. "Every time I think we'll learn something that will lead us to Helena, we run into a dead end," Henderson said.

Elle pulled out her phone. "We did learn some interesting facts, though. Now that we have a full picture of the snake tattoo, we can ask the sheriff's office to check it against known gang markings and I can send it to Sabina for our own searches. I don't know how she does it, but she can access all kinds of databases."

Henderson slowed to make a right turn onto the road leading to Twin Oaks. "Something about the Sonshine Co-op sounds familiar to me."

Elle snapped a photo of the tattoo drawing and sent it to Sabina with the request to find out more about it and the co-op. She slipped her phone back into her purse. "Did Helena mention it?"

"I can't recall her doing so, but I'll ask my mom when we get back."

Up ahead on the right-hand verge lay a crumpled mound that hadn't been there on their way in. "Be careful. Looks like some roadkill isn't all the way on the right shoulder."

He tapped the brakes as the SUV approached.

Elle realized her mistake all at once. "Stop the car!"

Henderson slammed on the brakes, bringing the vehicle to a stop a few feet ahead of the body. "What's the matter?"

She unbuckled her seat belt and wrenched open the door. "It's not an animal—it's a child!"

TEN

Henderson threw the gear into Park and raced after Elle, who had dropped to her knees beside the prone figure of a child, who lay on his—her?—side. He crouched opposite her.

"His heartbeat is racing and his skin is flushed and dry," Elle said.

Henderson struggled to recall his first-aid training. "I think that might mean heatstroke. I'll get some water from the SUV."

He ran to the vehicle and grabbed both of their half-empty water bottles, along with an old, clean towel he kept for emergencies. More of his training came back to him. Possible heatstroke victims needed to be cooled off quickly. He started the vehicle, blasted the AC as high as it would go, and made his way back to Elle.

Over the child's head, Elle waved her hands to create a breeze. Henderson soaked the towel and placed it on the child's forehead. "We need to cool him off in the car. Can you tell if he has any other injuries?"

The child's eyelids fluttered as Elle checked his limbs. "Everything seems okay. Should we call for an ambulance?"

Henderson punched in 9-1-1, quickly explaining their emergency to the dispatcher, who informed him an ambulance would take half an hour since the town's unit was responding to a farm accident at one of the orchards.

"Is he breathing?"

"Yes, I think he's suffering from heatstroke. There's no other obvious signs of trauma or bleeding, no scrapes or bruises," he said.

"Can you transport him to the clinic?" the dispatcher asked. "We'll send an ambulance there from another county."

"Yes, my car is right here."

"I'll alert them you're on your way," the dispatcher replied. "Keep the line open in case his condition worsens."

"Got it." Henderson slipped the phone into his back pocket then turned to Elle. "We're to take him to the clinic." He bent and slipped his arms under the child's legs and upper torso. "Get the back door for me."

Elle hurried ahead and opened the door as Henderson carried the child to the SUV. After laying the child on the seat, he repositioned the wet towel. "The clinic's only a couple of miles down the road. Can you sit with him in the back?"

Elle nodded as she took a seat beside him. Henderson jumped into the front seat and pulled onto the road, pushing the SUV above the speed limit. Within minutes, the Twin Oaks Medical Clinic came into view. Without bothering to find a parking space, he stopped in front of the awning-covered entrance.

By the time he exited the vehicle, Elle had the back door open. "I'll go in while you get the child."

Scooping up the boy, he walked as quickly as he could with his burden. Inside, a nurse beckoned him through the waiting room. Once in the back hallway, Elle stood talking to a woman in a white lab coat while a second nurse in dog-print scrubs pointed to an open examine room.

Henderson laid the child on the table just as the kid opened his eyes. For a moment, a sense of déjà vu washed over him as their gazes connected. The child had eyes the same warm brown as his sister's—the similarities jolting him to his core.

Then someone placed a hand on his shoulder, breaking the spell. The nurse in dog-print scrubs stood beside him. "Sir, if you'll step into the hallway, we'll take it from here."

Telling the 9-1-1 dispatcher they'd arrived at the clinic, Henderson ended the call as the nurse guided him from the room and into the hall, where Elle met him.

"Will he be okay?" Elle asked as another nurse pointed them in the direction of the waiting room.

"I don't know, but he's in good hands now."

Henderson joined her on a fabric-covered couch. The waiting room of the town's only urgent care facility was only half full. A mother bounced a squalling infant in her arms while a toddler played at her feet. An older woman sat beside a teenager, whose fingers flew over the keypad of his phone. A few other adults either gazed at their phones or watched the silent TV, which showed a home improvement program with subtitles.

The door to the clinic opened and a man walked in wearing dirty jeans, a faded T-shirt and a leather jacket that had seen better days. His gaze swept the room once and then he headed to the receptionist. "Where is she?"

From where Henderson sat, he had a visual of the young woman behind the plexiglass window, who smiled at the man. "Who are you looking for, sir?"

Her question appeared to irritate him because he leaned forward. "Where is Rose McCellan?" His voice rose. "I know she's here. What have you done with her?"

"Sir, are you a relative?" The receptionist held

on to her composure, but Henderson could see her tremble.

"She's my wife," the man replied. "I'm not going to ask again."

"What's going on?" A man in a white lab coat, a stethoscope around his neck, stepped into the waiting room.

"I'll tell you what's going on. I want to see my wife." The man turned his anger on the newcomer.

"I'm sure we can get this straightened out. I'm Dr. Krist, Mr....?" The doctor's easy manner had the desired effect on the man, who visibly relaxed.

"Hank McCellan. I want to see my wife," Hank repeated, moving away from the reception window to stand only a few feet from Henderson and Elle.

Beside him, Elle whispered, "I think Hank's on something. See how dilated his pupils are?"

Henderson took in Hank's eyes. Sure enough, his pupils loomed huge, and his hands shook slightly.

"Mr. McCellan, your wife isn't here," Dr. Krist responded, his voice calm and measured. "She's been moved to the hospital in Harrisonburg."

Hank clenched his fists. "That's a lie. She's here. I dropped her off myself."

"And she was here on Sunday," the doctor said.

The words seemed to confuse Hank. "What are you talking about? I left her a few hours ago!"

Dr. Krist couldn't quite hide his alarm.

Henderson couldn't blame him. After all, it was Wednesday. Henderson touched Elle's arm, pitching his voice low. "We should move in case this turns ugly."

She nodded her agreement, but Hank side-stepped right in front of their chairs, sending a whiff of foul odor into Henderson's nostrils. The man's jittery movements and unkempt appearance brought to mind druggie clients he'd had as a public defender. Henderson tensed, his eyes never leaving Hank.

"Rose! I'm coming for you!" Hank reached behind him under his jacket and drew a gun from the waistband of his jeans.

Henderson tensed, his entire body coiled and ready to defend the woman beside him and the others in the waiting room. *Please God, keep them safe.* The prayer calmed his nerves, but he wouldn't let down his guard, not with the unpredictableness of a man both grieving and likely high on drugs pacing in front of him with a weapon in his hand.

As Hank aimed the handgun at the doctor, fear rose like a fast tide inside Elle. She had encountered someone high on cocaine while on a community ride-along with the police a few years ago, and the unpredictability of that man's actions had frightened her, even in the presence of law enforcement. Here, no one stood between her and danger.

"Mr. McCellan, Rose isn't here. She's at the hospital," Dr. Krist repeated, his manner calm. "Please put the gun away before someone gets hurt."

Hank shook his head. "No, no, no, no. All lies! She's here. I dropped her off right when the clinic opened today. She can't have been moved so quickly."

Clearly, something had made the man lose several days and, based on his actions, Elle suspected drugs.

"Your wife suffered from an overdose of methamphetamine," Dr. Krist said. "She was in bad shape when she arrived."

Hank froze, his eyes widening. "What? No, Rose never took too much. It couldn't have been an overdose."

The doctor's countenance grew troubled. "Her symptoms lined up with a drug overdose."

"You're lying. Why do you keep lying?" Hank slowly turned, aiming his gun at various patients until he faced Elle and Henderson. His wild eyes raked over her. Elle shrank back in her seat, resisting the urge to cover her eyes to avoid that penetrating stare.

Hank grabbed her upper arm, his fingers biting into her flesh as he pulled her to her feet. He jammed the gun against her side, digging the muzzle into her ribs hard enough to bring tears to her eyes. "Now tell me the truth. Where is my wife?"

"May I get out my phone to call the hospital?" Dr. Krist held up his hands in front of him, sweat glistening on his upper lip and forehead. "Perhaps you could talk to your wife or see her on a video chat."

Hank considered the question for so long, Elle thought he must have forgotten what the doctor had asked. Then he nodded, but didn't release Elle.

Dr. Krist gingerly pulled out his phone and dialed a number. "This Dr. Krist at the Twin Oaks clinic. I'd like to check on a patient sent by ambulance three days ago. Rose McCellan."

Elle moved her arm in an effort to get Hank to loosen his grasp, but her action backfired when instead he tightened his fingers.

The doctor's face paled and Elle's heartrate skyrocketed.

"I see," Dr. Krist said, his eyes on Elle's face. In their depths, she read grief and fear. "Would you connect me please?"

"What's taking so long? Why aren't you getting Rose on the phone?" Hank stepped closer to the doctor, dragging Elle along with him.

"I'm working on it," Dr. Krist said. "She's been moved to a different floor of the hospital."

Elle greatly feared she knew which floor—

the basement, where most hospitals had their morgues.

"Yes, Dr. Krist calling about Rose McCellan. I have her husband in my clinic and he wants to see his wife." Dr. Krist's voice didn't convey that Hank held a gun to a hostage. Elle doubted she could have spoken so calmly if their situations had been reversed.

The doctor's tone dropped lower and then he disconnected the phone.

"Why'd you do that?" Hank jabbed the gun in the doctor's direction. "I want to see Rose!"

"The hospital is calling back on a video call so you can see her." Dr. Krist's phone jangled and he swiped across the screen. "This is Dr. Krist. I have Hank McClellan with me, Rose's husband."

Hank craned his neck to see the doctor's phone. Elle suspected Dr. Krist held it deliberately as far away as possible to get the man to come closer. As Hank shifted to see the phone, his fingers relaxed a bit on Elle's arm. She eased to the side a few centimeters and turned her head to see what was happening behind them in the waiting room.

A nurse directed patients to a side door, out of sight from Hank. The room had emptied of most who had been waiting, except for Henderson and an elderly couple sitting nearly opposite Hank.

From the corner of her eye, she caught a glimpse of Henderson standing slowly. Then Hank crushed her backward into him, sliding his arm across her neck in one swift movement. "No! She can't be dead!"

Hank raised the gun at the doctor, his other arm pressing down against her windpipe. "You killed her! You took her from me and killed her!"

As Hank heaved her upward, spots danced in front of Elle's eyes. She strained to stay on her tiptoes to relieve some of the pressure on her throat, but Hank's taller frame and his frantic movements left her scrambling to keep upright.

"I have nothing without her! Nothing!" Hank's anguished cry echoed throughout the room.

The sound rang in Elle's ears as she gasped for air. Her vision dimmed as if someone had turned down the lights.

Then a loud boom of a gunshot pierced the air.

ELEVEN

Henderson let go of Hank's arm as the man released his hold on Elle and dropped to the floor, clutching a gunshot wound in his leg. Dr. Krist fell on his knees beside the injured man, while Elle staggered against Henderson. Holding her close, he thanked God he'd been able to force the man's hand downward before Hank shot himself in the temple.

"It's okay. I've got you." He led Elle to a chair, sinking into one beside her while Dr. Krist leaned over Hank, his hands pressing down on the bleeding wound.

Elle bent over, drawing in huge gulps of air, her body heaving as it replenished oxygen into her bloodstream and lungs. Henderson rubbed her back as the room filled with deputies, who waved in EMTs after securing Hank's weapon.

An EMT knelt in front of Elle. "What happened?"

Henderson recapped the events as the EMT

placed a portable oxygen mask on Elle and took her vitals. "Is she going to be okay?"

"She should get a thorough checkup at the hospital to be sure," he replied. "The clinic will be a crime scene for a while."

Henderson took in her pale complexion and the red mark on her neck, agreeing with the assessment.

Two other EMTs loaded Hank onto a gurney and wheeled him out of the clinic.

"Will he live?" Henderson was glad he'd been able to foil Hank's attempt to commit suicide.

"I think so," Dr. Krist said, his face grim. "I'm sorry. I thought seeing his wife would calm him, not wind him up."

"Druggies are even more unpredictable than the general population," Henderson said.

The doctor's shoulders slumped. "It's the meth. For several months, we've had an uptick in drug overdoses and accidents related to meth usage. I know the sheriff's office is working on finding the source, but it's like trying to hit a moving target." He touched Henderson's arm. "Again, I'm sorry."

"It was a tough call to make," Henderson said, meaning it. He might not have made the choice to show Hank his dead wife's face, but he couldn't entirely fault Dr. Krist for thinking that might make Hank collapse in grief—and release Elle unharmed.

"Here's your ride." The EMT repacked his supplies as a colleague brought another gurney alongside Elle.

Her eyes grew wide above the oxygen mask.

Henderson placed his hand over hers, surprised by how cold her fingers were. "Does she have to ride in the ambulance?"

"It would be best so we can monitor her breathing and keep the oxygen flowing," the first responder said.

"I'll follow right behind you," Henderson assured her.

Elle allowed the EMTs to help her onto the gurney as Deputy Stubbs stepped up beside them. "We meet again."

Henderson thought he detected annoyance in the deputy's tone but he shoved that to the back of his mind when Elle plucked Henderson's sleeve and removed her mask. "What about the child?"

Henderson explained to the deputy as the EMTs strapped Elle onto the stretcher. "We brought in a kid we found by the side of the road. Heatstroke we thought. Can you see if he's okay?"

"He's probably been transported to the hospital, but I'll try to find out and let you know what I can," Stubbs said. "I'll be in touch for your statements once we're finished here."

Henderson thanked the deputy and trailed the EMTs and Elle outside. After confirming the hospital's location in Harrisonburg, about an hour away, he jumped into his SUV and followed the ambulance to the hospital, a prayer of thanksgiving for Elle's safety and one for the child's recovery on his lips.

Once at the hospital, he found a chair in the waiting area. With signs encouraging limited cell phone conversations, he put off updating his mom and scrolled through his email instead. An hour later, he stopped by the front desk in response to a text from Elle.

"Hi, Elle Updike asked me to go back." He waited while the older man verified his identity and handed him a visitor's badge. Thanking him, Henderson followed his directions to find Elle's cubicle on the far rim of the bustling emergency department. He poked his head around the partially closed curtain. "Hey, how are you?"

She sat with her legs dangling over the side. "Ready to get out of here."

He winced at her raspy voice. "How's your throat?"

"Like I swallowed sandpaper, but better once they sprayed it with some painkillers." She swung her leg. "The nurse said she'd be right back with my discharge papers. Any word on the child's condition?"

"The deputy hasn't updated me." Privately, he wasn't sure Stubbs would even remember the request, given all that was on the deputy's plate. From where he stood at the curtain's edge, he caught a glimpse of a slim figure with long brown hair out of the corner of his eye. Something about the woman reminded him of his sister. "Be right back."

Henderson hurried in the direction the woman had gone, sidestepping medical personnel and visitors, but he lost her in the busy ER. Frowning, he pivoted in a slow circle, scanning each face. Not seeing the woman, he walked the perimeter, discretely glancing in every cubicle that didn't have the curtains tightly drawn. Discouragement beat down on him as he made his way back to Elle without finding her.

Parting the curtain to her bed, he took one last look around the ER before facing Elle. His stomach dropped at the sight of his quarry standing with her back to him, talking to Elle. His heart-rate zoomed and his vision blurred. "Helena?"

The word came out as a whisper as the woman turned. For one brief crazy moment, he envisioned his sister there beside Elle's gurney. Then his vision cleared and the features of a stranger resolved on the woman's face. He pressed the heels of his hands into his eyes, despair strangling his vocal chords.

"Henderson?"

Drawing air deep into his lungs, he lowered his hands to gaze into Elle's concerned eyes. "Sorry, long day." A lame excuse that, by the look in her eyes, she hadn't bought, but to his relief, Elle didn't call him on the lie.

"This is Nalani Judd, the mother of the boy we found," Elle said.

Nalani smiled, a dimple appearing on her right cheek. Her brown eyes flecked with green held fast on his. "I can't thank you enough, Mr. Parker, for what you and Elle did to help my son, Holden."

"Please call me Henderson," he said automatically as the boy's name brought another stab of grief. Helena had become obsessed with the name after reading J. D. Salinger's *The Catcher in the Rye* in high school, swearing she'd name her son after the narrator. "How's he doing?"

Nalani clapped her hands together. "He'll make a full recovery, thanks to you both. The doctors want to keep him overnight for observation. You can't be too careful with heatstroke in children."

"What was he doing on that road?" Elle asked.

"Having an adventure, I'm sure." Nalani shrugged her shoulders. "Boys will be boys."

"Knock, knock." A nurse pulled back the curtain and entered with a sheaf of papers in her hand. "I've got your discharge papers, Ms. Updike."

"That's my cue to leave," Nalani said. "Thank you both so much." Her countenance grew troubled. "I'm only sorry that your helping Holden resulted in your injuries, Elle."

"I'll be okay. We're just glad we were able to

help." Elle signed the papers as Nalani slipped out of the cubicle.

Later, as he walked with Elle to his SUV, Henderson ran the encounter over in his mind, trying to put his finger on what bothered him. Something about Nalani Judd had tickled his subconscious, but for the life of him, he couldn't bring it into focus. He only knew they were no closer to finding Helena than he'd been when he'd arrived in Twin Oaks.

"What was that all about?" Elle waited until Henderson had pointed the SUV toward Tall Trees before voicing the question that had been burning in her mind ever since he'd left her cubicle. The expression on his face when he'd first seen Nalani made her think he'd seen a ghost. He'd said something, but too softly for her to catch. Then it was as if he'd shaken himself like a dog after a dip in the lake and was back to being the Henderson she'd come to know.

"What was what all about?" Henderson tightened his grip on the steering wheel, his posture giving lie to the casualness of his question.

She blew out a breath. "Don't play games with me. You left, and when you returned, you were blindsided by Nalani's presence. Explain yourself. Please."

Henderson braked for a traffic light and glanced her way. The pain in his eyes touched her heart. "I thought I saw Helena."

"Oh, Henderson." She touched his shoulder as the light turned green and he accelerated. "And it was Nalani Judd?"

He nodded, his lips firming into a thin line. "Yes, I caught a glimpse of her moving around the ER—I guess she was looking for you. Her hair is the same shade and style as Helena's was the last time I saw my sister."

"I'm so sorry." He hadn't wanted to tell the story of his last meeting with Helena during their earlier recording session. She pulled out her phone and opened the recording app. "Would you tell me about your final encounter with Helena?"

He flicked his gaze to her and his eyes widened at the sight of the phone in her hand. "For the podcast?"

She winced, reminding herself his grief and disappointment were likely the reason for his harsh tone. "Yes, and because I think it might help us find her."

He hit the heel of his hand on the steering wheel. "Every time I think we have a lead, it turns out to be dust in the wind."

"I know." And she did, her mind flashing back to the second season of *Gone*, where she'd tried to help a family find a missing child but all their hard work had led to nothing. She still held out hope that a future listener to the podcast would come forward with the missing piece of evidence that would lead to the child.

"Go ahead and turn that thing on." His jaw muscles twitched. He waited until she indicated he could begin. "It was in November, right before Thanksgiving. It will be nine years this fall."

He cleared his throat. Elle prayed he would have the strength to relive the memory.

"I had just started working in the public defender's office, much to my dad's disapproval. He'd wanted me to join the district attorney's office from the get-go because he knew the DA personally—golfing buddy. But I wanted to be my own man and…well, ended up on the other side of things. Seems petty now, but it was in defending low-life drug dealers, deadbeat dads, prostitutes and the occasional murderer that I fell in love with the law, saw it in all its beauty and sorrows."

Elle held her breath as he described some of his early cases, hearing both the joy and discouragement of his job.

"Then one day I got a call from Helena, out of the blue. I hadn't heard from her in months, despite my attempts to connect. Always got her voicemail or no answer to my calls or texts." He pointed to a road sign indicating a popular chain convenience store and gas station. "I need to fill up and get a snack."

She hit Stop on the recording as her stomach growled. "Food sounds good. I think we missed dinner." The dashboard clock read 7:03. No wonder she suddenly felt like she could eat an elephant.

As Henderson signaled his intention to take the next exit, a dark blue pickup with huge wheels eased up behind them. Elle frowned. Hadn't she seen the monster truck in the parking lot of the hospital? She watched in the passenger's-side mirror as the truck followed them off the highway. When the driver pulled into the gas station island opposite them, the vise around her chest eased. Just another motorist who needed fuel, like them.

After Henderson filled up, he moved the SUV to a parking spot and they purchased hot subs and cold fountain drinks, eating at one of the outside picnic tables. A cooling breeze stirred the hot air, bringing with it a whiff of rain. Elle shielded her eyes against the setting sun to see fat rain clouds on the horizon. "Looks like rain is coming."

Henderson assessed the sky and checked the weather app on his phone. "According to this, we should make it back to the B and B before the storm comes."

Elle finished her sub, wadding up the paper. "I hope so." She gathered Henderson's empty wrapper. "Ready?"

"Let's roll," he said, grabbing his soda. She tossed the trash then snagged the rest of her diet drink. The cold carbonation eased the soreness of her throat.

Back on the highway, Elle turned to Henderson. "Want to resume your story?"

"Sure."

She restarted the recording.

"Helena had gotten herself picked up for drug possession, and remembered her brother was a lawyer." His tone held a mixture of bitterness and pity. "Of course, I went there right away."

Elle glanced in the mirror to see if the blue pickup had followed them back onto the highway. The gloam made it harder to see if the truck was among the vehicles crowding the interstate. As Henderson recounted his visit with Helena in the city jail and his sister's belligerence and insistence she hadn't done anything wrong, her heart broke at the pain in his voice.

"I managed to get the charge knocked down to a misdemeanor with probation. She kissed my cheek and said…"

His voice trailing off yanked Elle's attention from the side mirror. "What?"

"I just remembered why Sonshine Co-op sounded so familiar to me."

"Why?" Her reporter's instinct quivered.

"The last time I saw her, I asked if I could drop her off somewhere. She shook her finger at me, saying she didn't want me to know where she was staying because I'd eventually tell Dad, and he'd swoop in and ruin her life." A sad smile crossed his face. "Which, of course, was exactly what would have happened. She said a friend would be picking her up. I wanted to wait with her on the sidewalk outside the courthouse, but had another court appearance in ten minutes with a judge who didn't tolerate tardiness."

Elle leaned toward him, her hand holding the phone steady, her heart beating wildly. Maybe this would be the break they needed.

"I turned to go when her ride pulled up." His gaze met Elle's. "It was a van with the words Sonshine Landscaping on it."

She didn't believe in coincidences. It might not be enough to launch an official investigation by the sheriff's department, but in her book, the similar names meant they were on the right track. Sonshine Co-op would bear closer scrutiny—and possibly lead them to Helena.

TWELVE

Henderson signaled his intention to exit the interstate, scanning the traffic as he maneuvered the SUV onto the ramp.

"Did you tell the police about the van when you reported her missing?" Elle's voice still had a husky timbre, which the ER doctor said might last a few days.

He braked at the stop sign, glancing into the rearview mirror. A dark pickup, its carriage jacked up so high, its headlights reflecting off the shiny surface hit him square in the eyes. Before replying, he flipped the mirror to avoid the bright lights. "I know I talked about the van and mentioned the landscaping company name, but since I could only give a generic description of the vehicle—and the New York license plate had been obscured by mud—they couldn't locate it. Or the company. Said no company by that name had a business license in the state."

"A dead end."

He drummed his fingers along the top of the steering wheel as they left the interstate commerce behind on the two-lane highway that would take them to Twin Oaks. His mind turned over how the old information could fit into their present circumstances. "Sonshine Co-op is pretty generic, even spelled with an *o* instead of a *u*, but I don't like coincidences."

"Me either." Elle twisted in her seat to glance behind them. "Did you see a blue, jacked-up pickup behind us when you exited?"

His pulse increased. "I did." He paused, not sure he wanted to know the answer to his next question. "Why?"

"I think it's following us." She faced the front again. "I thought I saw it in the hospital parking lot. I definitely spotted it when we pulled off for gas and dinner."

"That's one too many coincidences for me."

"Me too. Should I call the sheriff's office?"

"Unless the driver actually threatens us in some way, there's nothing the sheriff could do."

"Is it still behind us?"

He checked the mirrors but couldn't tell if the truck was among the vehicles trailing their SUV. "I can't tell. Can you check again?"

She leaned forward, her head tilted away from his. "I'm not sure. The headlights make it difficult to see."

The anxiety in her voice made him want to tug

her into his arms. That was ridiculous. His focus had to stay on finding Helena. He had failed to find his sister while his father was alive, and he had to ensure his mother would see her daughter again before she died. He doubted Elle knew about Kathleen's weak heart—his mother had been firm in her insistence that Henderson keep her illness to himself. All the more reason for him to not get distracted by a pair of blue eyes, no matter how much his heart urged him.

Maybe he wasn't capable of love. That's what Janice had accused him of when she'd broken their engagement. "All you care about is finding your missing sister." What he'd wanted to respond was that he had put searching for Helena on the back burner with Janice, only she hadn't seen it that way. When Janice had eloped with her college sweetheart, his heart had been hurt. Recently, he'd suspected the ache had had more to do with his injured pride than his feelings for Janice, which made her accusation more believable.

As they passed more communities, the line of cars behind them dwindled until only two remained. Henderson suspected the dark pickup lingered behind a sedan, its headlights beaming over the top of the lower car. "I think the pickup is two cars behind us."

Elle glanced in the side mirror. "Oh, no, the other car is signaling a left turn."

Henderson gripped the wheel more tightly as

the barrier between them and the pickup disappeared. No headlights illuminated the oncoming traffic lane, leaving them and the truck the only vehicles on the darkened road. "I don't like this. Get ready to call 9-1-1."

She held up her phone. "Just got to hit the call button."

When a couple of miles passed with the truck staying three car lengths behind, he heaved a sigh of relief. "Maybe we both overreacted and—"

The roar of an engine drowned out his words as the pickup swerved into the lane beside them and accelerated until it hovered even with their vehicle. Henderson spared a quick look out his window, but the darkness hid the driver's features. "Can you see who's in the truck?"

"No," she said, angling over the back seat to see out the driver's-side windows. "It's too dark."

A bright light flooded the interior of the SUV, nearly blinding him. "What's going on?"

Elle shielded her eyes. "They're shining a spotlight into our car."

Henderson pressed down on the accelerator and the SUV shot forward, darkness bathing the interior once more. But the pickup soon rode alongside them again, the bright light once again distorting his vision. "I can't see the road clearly."

She leaned down, rummaging in her bag before extracting a piece of cloth. "I have an extra

T-shirt I can use to block your window. I'm going to climb in the back seat."

Before he could object, she had unbuckled her seat belt and climbed over the middle console and into the back. While she worked on a solution, he struggled to keep his eyes—and SUV—on the road, as it twisted and turned. Finally, the brightness faded as Elle secured the T-shirt over his window. "Is that better?"

"Yes, thanks." The light still annoyed him, but it wasn't as potentially dangerous to nighttime driving now.

Then he spotted headlights in the distance, heading toward them.

"There's a car coming towards us," Elle gasped from behind him.

"Buckle up." He kept an eye on the pickup in the lane next to them as the oncoming vehicle zipped closer.

"It's a semi!"

Surely the pickup wasn't going to play chicken with a tractor-trailer. Henderson had no intention of being collateral damage in that game. He floored the gas and the SUV leaped forward as the speedometer crept past eighty. The truck dropped behind, slipping into the lane just as the semi roared past.

Henderson eased back on the pedal when a road sign indicating curve ahead flashed by. As the SUV went into the turn, the pickup slammed into the rear end, sending them spinning across the road—directly into the path of another vehicle.

Elle squeezed her eyes shut, fully expecting to hear the crunch of metal on metal and feel the impact of another vehicle hitting theirs. When the only sound was the blaring of horns and the screech of brakes, accompanied by a gunning engine, she pried open her eyes to see the world had stopped spinning—and the SUV rested perpendicular to the road.

"You okay?" Henderson twisted in his seat to see behind him.

"Yeah. What just happened?" She looked around for her phone, which had slipped from her hand.

"I'm not sure." He blew out a long breath, his hands still hanging on to the steering wheel so tight, his knuckles had turned white.

"Hey, we're okay." She gently touched his shoulder.

A knock on the rear window sent her heart-rate back into the stratosphere. A man wearing a baseball cap and overalls stood outside. Beyond him, running lights illuminated a small truck sitting on the shoulder.

She depressed the power button to lower the window.

"You two okay?" a familiar voice asked.

Elle squinted in the darkness to discern the man's features. Recognition relaxed her shoulders. "Howard Gray?"

The man leaned over, bringing his face level with hers. "Ms. Updike, Mr. Parker? What are you doing out here?" Then he straightened to look around before bending down again. "You'd best get your vehicle out of the road. There's a historical marker pull-off area just around the curve. I'll meet you there."

Without waiting to see if they would comply, Gray jogged back to his truck. Henderson turned the steering wheel and guided the vehicle to the designated spot before cutting the engine. After removing the T-shirt from the window, he leaned against the headrest. "That was way too close for comfort."

Elle murmured her agreement, her mind flashing back to the close call as a tremor jolted her body. They could have been killed or badly injured by the blue pickup's aggressive driving.

Gray parked behind them and got out of his truck.

"Some fresh air will help." Henderson opened his door then assisted her from the back seat.

She looked down at her shaking hands. "Delayed reaction, I guess."

"Hey, it will be okay." He lightly brushed his fingertips across her cheek, smoothing back several strands of hair.

Her legs gave way as the full extent of what had almost happened hit her, and she slumped into his solid frame. He easily absorbed her weight, wrapping an arm firmly around her waist as he shut the door. Then he put both arms around her, one hand rubbing up and down her spine. The comforting rhythm broke the hold Elle had on her emotions and tears spilled over her cheeks. With a sigh, she leaned her head against his chest, her fingers bunching the fabric of his T-shirt. The stress of the near-accident, coupled with the events of the day, had pushed her to her emotional limit. But instead of feeling drained, like she usually did after such a crying jag, her soul wasn't as ragged and raw. Having a strong shoulder to cry on helped to ease her burden. Her mind told her not to put too much stock in those feelings, but her heart nudged her to consider how much of her comfort came from the fact it was Henderson Parker offering it.

"Better?" Henderson's lips brushed her hair as he spoke.

Mentally, she gave herself a good shake and then stepped out of his arms. "Yes, thank you. Guess the events of the day caught up with me." She wiped the remaining tears from her face with her fingers.

"Use this." He pressed a handkerchief into her hands.

"Thanks." She tried to smile but gave up when

her lips wobbled too much. Discretely wiping mascara from under her eyes, she blew her nose then faced the two men. "Sorry about that," she said to Gray.

"No need to apologize." He flashed a quick smile. "My wife's always bursting into tears at the drop of a hat, says those pregnancy hormones make her emotions hover right below the surface. Don't tell her, but it's not carrying our baby that's making her more emotional—she's always been a crier."

His confession, delivered with a wink and a tone leaving no doubt of his love for Milly, broke the ice and they all shared a chuckle. Then Gray sobered. "I thought for sure we were going to have a head-on collision. What happened?"

Henderson detailed the movements of the blue pickup, adding Elle's observation it had followed them from the hospital. "We have no idea why someone would want to run us off the road, but we're glad no one was injured."

"It was a close one." Gray removed his baseball cap and ran his fingers through his hair. "If I hadn't known the road so well, I wouldn't have been able to avoid hitting you straight-on. As it was, I swerved onto the shoulder in the nick of time."

"And we're glad you did," Elle put in, another shudder rippling through her at the memory. Henderson wrapped his arm around her shoulders, hugging her close.

"Will you report this to the sheriff's office?" Gray asked.

"Not sure," Henderson said. "We have a vague description of the vehicle, the front license plate had mud obscuring the letters or numbers, and no one was hurt."

Gray walked to the back of the SUV. "You do have some damage to your bumper, where it looks like the truck hit you."

Henderson squeezed Elle's shoulders before joining Gray at the rear of the vehicle. "Looks like there's some paint from the truck too. I'll call it in when we get back to the B and B."

After thanking Gray for his assistance, he restarted the truck's engine and pointed the vehicle toward Twin Oaks. While Gray seemed assured of the sheriff's cooperation in investigating the hit-and-run, Elle wasn't convinced it would be enough to connect the vehicle incident with their search for Helena. All she knew for sure was that their investigation was ruffling somebody's feathers, which was all the confirmation she needed to keep pressing for answers.

THIRTEEN

As Henderson parked at Tall Trees, a crack of thunder boomed, followed by a flash of lightening. The weather mirrored his seesawing emotions when it came to the woman beside him. The events of the day had ignited his protective instincts about Elle. When he'd held her against his chest while she'd sobbed, an overwhelming feeling of contentment had overtaken his senses.

"Storm's coming," she said, unbuckling her seat belt. "We'd better make a run for the house before we're drenched."

The security lights played across her face. His eyes traced the contours that had become more familiar and precious to him lately. Then rain began pounding the roof. "Too late."

"Is it?" Her husky voice made his insides tumble together like wrestlers on a mat.

He swayed toward her. "It's raining pretty hard."

"But it's nice and dry in here."

He cupped her cheek with his hand. "That it is." Another time, he would have berated himself for the stupidity of his reply, but in this moment, all he could think about was how smooth her skin felt underneath his fingers.

Her eyes slid closed as she leaned into his touch. He started when her fingers trailed along his beard. He touched his lips to her cheek.

"Henderson?"

"Hmm?" He feathered a kiss across the bridge of her nose as she placed her hands on either side of his face, stopping him. He gazed into her blue eyes, the warmth in them matching his own.

"I'd rather you kiss me like this." And she brought her lips full on his.

All thoughts about pickup trucks and his missing sister faded as he kissed Elle. The storm continued to dump torrents of water from the sky but inside the SUV, his attention focused solely on the woman in his arms. His breathing sounded overly loud as he wrestled to bring his emotions under control.

Beside him, Elle touched her lips with her fingers. "That was…" She left the sentence unfinished.

"Quite," he said, unable to put his feelings into words either.

Overhead, the storm lessened, the rain coming in a steady stream rather than a deluge. "I think the thunderstorm's passing."

He peered out his window. "I think you're right. Shall we make a run for it?"

Her hand reached for the door handle. "Race you to the house." Before he could agree, she had her door open. Then her slim figure darted through the rain to the bed-and-breakfast.

With a laugh, Henderson ran after her, splashing through puddles. Under the covered porch entrance, he caught up with Elle. "You won."

"What's my prize?" The teasing note in her voice made him bold.

"Another kiss." He reached for her but the door opened behind her before he could set his lips on hers again.

Elle jumped back, her cheeks reddening in the porch light.

Alec backed out of the doorway, a large plastic bin in his arms. "Oh, hi. You two get caught in the storm?"

"Sort of." Henderson gave a brief recap of their adventures.

"Wow. Glad you two are all right." Alec hefted the bin. "I've got to put this in the car so I don't forget to drop it off at the animal shelter tomorrow. Isabella's been after me to take these old towels there for weeks."

Alec stepped off the porch and down the stairs toward a SUV with the Tall Trees B and B logo emblazoned on the doors. A light breeze blew rain temporarily over them, even under the shelter of the porch roof. Before Henderson could say anything, Elle shivered, her arms hugging herself around the middle. "I think a warm bath is calling my name. See you tomorrow."

Henderson bid her good-night then turned to find Alec returning.

"She's very pretty," Alec observed as the two entered the house.

Henderson was saved from answering when his phone rang, the ringtone indicating his mother was calling. "It's my mom."

Alec said good-night and disappeared into the back of the house while Henderson climbed the stairs.

"Hey, Mom."

"Henderson Parker?"

He paused halfway up the stairs at the unfamiliar voice. "Yes, who's this?"

"I'm Mrs. Hundshamer, a social worker at Buffalo General Hospital."

"Is my mom all right?" Henderson sagged against the railing, his heart thumping so loudly he was sure the woman would hear it.

"Is Kathleen Parker your mother?" Mrs. Hundshamer replied. After he affirmed she was, the social worker continued. "Mrs. Parker was brought in few hours ago after she collapsed in the grocery store."

Henderson closed his eyes, winging a prayer for his mother's safety. "How is she?"

"She's resting comfortably."

"Was it her heart?" His mom had dismissed concerns over her heart condition for so many years, he had begun to think it as benign as she claimed.

"The doctors think she might have suffered a mild heart attack. They're running some tests to get a definitive answer. She asked that we get in touch with you." The woman cleared her throat. "Mrs. Parker said you have her medical power of attorney."

"That's correct, as well as her legal power of attorney." He pushed off the railing and took the remaining steps two at a time. "I'll be there as soon as I can catch a flight from Virginia."

He grabbed a few essentials from his room, then raced back to his rental to head to the airport. Driving through the diminishing rainstorm, he berated himself for becoming distracted by a pair of fetching blue eyes. His mother's health depended on his finding Helena—he wouldn't allow himself to forget that again.

Saturday morning, Elle closed the SUV door and walked around to join Isabella at the farmers market. Two days after the attack in the clinic, the bruises around her neck had morphed into a dark purple. Isabella had lent her a sleeveless summer turtleneck sweater to cover the worst of the bruises.

"Have you heard from Henderson?" Isabella unloaded a wagon from the back.

"Not since he texted me yesterday morning that he'd landed in Buffalo." Elle followed Isabella into the market, trying to wrestle her woebegone feelings at the silence from Henderson back into a box. She had promised herself years ago to not let anyone have the power to make her happy, given how little her own parents paid attention to her. Somehow, Henderson had slipped under her defenses and wormed his way into her heart.

"You must miss him," Isabella said, a knowing gleam in her eye.

Elle shrugged, turning away to finger a handbeaded purse for sale at one of the booths. To her relief, Isabella let the subject drop. For the next hour, Elle wandered through the vibrant market, sampling homemade breads, fresh apples and jams. Isabella filled the wagon with fresh produce and two large mums.

"Seen enough?" Isabella surveyed the market.

Elle nearly replied yes when she spotted a vendor with the sign Sonshine Co-op near the end of a row. "Are they regulars at the market?"

Isabella shaded her eyes to see where Elle pointed. "Sonshine Co-op?" When Elle nodded, Isabella pursed her lips. "Yes, they usually have a booth."

Elle sensed the other woman didn't like them.

"What's wrong with the co-op? It looks like they're doing a brisk business."

"That they are," Isabella said, her gaze speculative as she met Elle's eyes. "I think that's all I'll say until you meet them. Come on."

Elle and Isabella made their way to the booth, which anchored the far end of the market. The double space had a gleaming white canopy with a sunburst logo around Sonshine Co-op. Women in long skirts, their hair braided and pinned around their heads like a crown, waited on customers. Baskets of apples, Asian pears, beets, broccoli, cabbage, squash, tomatoes and peaches adorned the tables while soft panpipe music floated on the breeze.

Browsing the produce, Elle selected four peaches to purchase. She looked around for the end of the checkout line.

"May I put those in a bag for you?" A girl wearing a Sonshine Co-op T-shirt pushed her glasses back up onto the bridge of her nose as she stared at Elle.

"Sure." Elle handed the peaches to the child, who wrapped them in some sort of tissue-like paper before nestling them inside a net bag. "I like your hair." She pointed to the girl's blond hair done in a fishtail braid across her head.

The girl dipped her head, a shy smile flitting across her face. "Thank you."

"Hazel!" A woman wearing a half apron

placed her hand on the girl's shoulder. "Don't bother the customers."

The woman's harsh tone sounded out of proportion to Elle's ears. "She wasn't bothering me at all."

The woman firmed her lips, her eyes flicking from Elle to Hazel. "Go help Jeb with the apples."

The girl gave Elle the bag with the peaches and scurried off toward the back of the tent to where an older man sorted apples into baskets.

"Ready to check out?" the woman asked.

"Not yet. I'd like to look around a bit more," Elle said, her mind mulling over the exchange.

The woman didn't budge. "I think that's all you need today." She snatched the bag from Elle's fingers and marched over to a scale and cash box.

Elle raised her eyebrows at the woman's rudeness but followed her over to the checkout.

"That'll be five dollars." The woman crossed her arms, her glare hot enough to sizzle steaks.

Without a word, Elle slapped a five-dollar bill on the counter and took her bag. She was still puzzling over the exchange when she found Isabella waiting a few stalls down.

"Well?" Isabella pulled the wagon while Elle related what had happened.

At the SUV, she helped Isabella unload their purchases. "I think I see what you mean about the co-op. Everything's shiny and bright on the outside, but there's an undercurrent of something I can't quite put my finger on."

"Exactly. I knew you'd sense it." Isabella closed the back and they climbed into the vehicle. Heading for the B and B, she added, "Alec thinks I'm imagining things, but I'm not."

Elle stared out the window at the passing scenery, her mind dissecting the encounter. "The woman was rude to me, practically shoved me out of the booth."

Isabella turned into the driveway to Tall Trees. "I wonder why."

"All I can think of is that Hazel, the little girl who wrapped my peaches, wasn't supposed to help customers."

Isabella cut the engine. "Seems strange to take that out on the customers."

"Yeah, not a good vibe at all from Sonshine Co-op."

"Besides, I think they buy their produce from the big-box store in Harrisonburg."

That brought Elle up short. "What?" She extracted her bag of peaches and took one out. "These aren't homegrown?"

Isabella brought out a peach she had purchased from another vendor. "See how bright and vibrant the colors are on this one compared to yours? And yours looks absolutely perfect."

"While yours is a bit lopsided." Elle could see the differences now that Isabella had pointed them out. "Why would they try to pass off store-bought fruit as from their own orchard?"

"I can't say for sure, but probably because they're not really farming the land. Not seriously," Isabella retorted. "I don't know what they're doing, but my guess would be something they don't want anyone else to know."

Elle made a mental note to ask Sabina to dig deeper into Sonshine Co-op's background and find out what they might be hiding. If her hunch was correct, whatever they uncovered might lead them directly to Helena.

FOURTEEN

Henderson cranked up the AC, directing a vent to blow on his face in the hope that the frigid air would keep him alert on his drive to Tall Trees. He'd managed to catch an early evening flight from Buffalo Niagara International Airport to Shenandoah Valley Regional Airport with several plane changes along the way, arriving at his final destination at 3:00 a.m.

His mother had suffered a mild heart attack and had ordered him back to Virginia to search for Helena. His mother's sister, Kallie, had driven up from Connecticut to stay a few weeks with Kathleen, alleviating his mind about leaving his mom so soon after her health scare. "It will help my recovery much better to know you're hunting down every lead to find your sister," his mom had told him before kissing his cheek and sending him on his way.

Her faith in his success should have buoyed his spirits, but instead his thoughts had centered on Elle, who had become important to him in a such a short time. During his flights, his mind had drifted to her laugh and the way the sunlight brought out the highlights in her brown hair. Her brown eyes sparkling with excitement over another clue to Helena's whereabouts. Their kiss in the SUV after the truck had nearly run them off the road.

Only ten more miles to go. The weatherman informed listeners that Sunday would prove to be a more mild day, with temperatures rising only to the low eighties with a light breeze and plenty of sunshine. "It's going to be a great day to enjoy the outdoors, so grab your best gal or guy for a picnic or hike," the DJ said before segueing into another pop song.

Maybe he could tempt Elle into a picnic on the grounds of the B and B. He'd noticed a small wooded area with a path that led from the backyard. Thoughts of a lazy Sunday afternoon flitted through his mind as he pulled into the bed-and-breakfast's parking lot, cutting the engine. As he picked up his phone, a series of texts from his aunt popped up, sending his pulse into overdrive. Somehow, delivery must have been delayed, because the first one had a time stamp right before the first leg of his flights.

7:35 p.m.: Kathleen had another heart attack, this one more serious. Got her to the hospital in time.

9:40 p.m.: Doctors running more tests, think she has a blocked artery.

11:23 p.m.: Doctors determined she has a blocked artery. Prepping her for open-heart surgery in the morning.

1:19 a.m.: Saw Kathleen. She's resting comfortably. Said to tell you to find Helena, top priority. Loves you and is praying for your success.

3:10 a.m.: Surgery scheduled for 7:00 a.m. Kathleen's sleeping.

Seeing his aunt had texted last only a few minutes ago, he dialed her number.

"Aunt Kallie?"

"Henderson, you're back in Virginia?" His aunt sounded exhausted.

"Yes, just arrived at the B and B in Twin Oaks." He paused. "I'll turn around and head back to the airport."

"No!" Kallie sighed. "Your mother doesn't want you here when you're chasing down leads about Helena."

He pinched the bridge of his nose. "I should be there with her."

"You know your mother," Kallie said. "She about bit my head off when I suggested your place was at her side." Her voice softened. "Finding your sister will be the best medicine and will help her recovery more than all the care the hospital can provide."

Tears pricked his eyes. "She's all I have left."

Kallie didn't answer for a moment. "She's in God's hands, like you are, like Helena is. Keep pressing on. Find Helena then bring your sister home. Let me pray for you."

While his aunt prayed, Henderson wiped a tear from his cheek, his emotions teetering on the brink. As Kallie invoked God's protection and His mercy on Henderson's search, he leaned his head against the seat, asking God in his heart to keep his mother safe.

"Thank you," he said when she'd finished.

"I'll update you after the surgery, but she won't be in recovery until two at the earliest."

They said their goodbyes and, for several minutes, he sat in the car. From now on, his focus had to be solely on discovering Helena's whereabouts—and most definitely not on how attractive he found Elle Updike. He'd have to make that clear to her later today, and only hope she wouldn't hear his own heart hurting when he did so.

Grabbing his overnight bag, he exited the vehicle then headed up the porch stairs only to find a new keypad lock on the door. A groan escaped. He'd forgotten Alec had mentioned the installation yesterday. He must have overlooked sending Henderson the combination.

Three thirty-one. Maybe they hadn't changed the lock to the kitchen or back door. He'd check first before texting Alec. No sense waking the man unless absolutely necessary. Carrying his bag, he circled the large house to the back door. A shiny new keypad lock met his gaze. With a sigh, he trudged to the kitchen door recessed slightly to the left of the rear entrance. Another brand-new lock had replaced the keyed dead bolt and handle.

Movement in his peripheral vision made Henderson step into the shadows. Four black-clad figures stood huddled together at the edge of the woods. He pulled out his cell phone, glad he'd kept the dark mode on for the GPS so the screen didn't light up and give away his hiding place. Should he shout in the hope the intruders would leave—for he had no doubt they had nefarious intentions—or call 9-1-1 and give away his position?

When the group fanned out, Henderson saw that each one held a bottle with a piece of fabric stuffed into the neck. Their tall builds suggested all were men. The furthest figure flicked a lighter and lit the end of the fabric wick, with the others following suit. Henderson stepped out of the shadows, preparing to tell the men to leave. As one of the figures reared his arm back to launch the first Molotov cocktail toward the house, a shot rang out.

The men froze, flames licking the fabric of their homemade bombs.

Alec stepped into the yard from the back door, racking another round in the shotgun he carried. "I've called the sheriff, and explained that my home was being invaded by four masked men carrying weapons." The former army captain advanced on the men. "The first shot was a warning to get off my property."

As if to underscore Alec's words, a siren split the silence. Three of the men turned to the figure on the far right, who hesitated a fraction of a minute. Then he smashed the bottle onto the edge of the patio. In the ensuing explosion, his companions threw their bottles on the grass, but none of their bottles broke. All the figures hightailed it back into the woods.

Henderson raced to the garden hose near the kitchen, turning on the spigot before unraveling the hose. He aimed the water at the intact bottles while Alec sprayed foam from a fire extinguisher on the burning petrol. Together, they managed to douse the flames and keep the fire from spreading.

"That was close," Henderson said.

"Too close." Alec's jaw tightened. "If I hadn't woken up and looked out the window, this could have ended much differently."

Sirens grew louder, accompanied by the sound of heavy vehicles on the gravel driveway. Soon firefighters raced around the corner of the house and took over, ensuring that nothing remained burning, and removing the unexploded Molotov cocktails.

A sheriff's deputy approached as lights began coming on inside the house. "You two seem to attract trouble," Deputy Stubbs said.

Alec shrugged. "Or trouble seems to follow us."

"Either way, you might want to consider doing something different." Stubbs surveyed the smoldering, black patches on the once manicured lawn. "They weren't fooling around."

"I think we must be getting close to finding Helena and—"

The deputy didn't let Henderson finish. "There is no evidence tying this incident—or any of the others—to your sister. She called your mother. Therefore, she's not missing."

Henderson opened his mouth to protest when Isabella joined her husband outside, Elle at her heels.

"Are you all right?" Isabella asked, wrapping her arms around her husband.

Elle touched Henderson's arm, her fingers feather-light on his bare skin. "You okay?"

He nodded. "They meant to burn the house down." His voice cracked as the realization of what had nearly happened flooded his body, kicking the adrenaline to the curb. Elle and the Stratmans might not have made it out alive.

"Let's go into the kitchen. I think a cup of something hot is needed." Isabella took charge, shepherding Henderson, Elle, Alec, and Stubbs through the kitchen door. Once inside, she made preparations for tea, while Alec went through the events of the night.

Stubbs took notes, peppering him and Henderson with questions. Henderson added his own observations.

Stubbs drained his mug. "Thank you for the tea, Mrs. Stratman. If you think of anything else to add, please let me know." He rose, cramming his hat back on his head. "And please, stay out of trouble, would you?"

Alec walked the deputy to the door while Isabella tidied the tea things.

Elle turned to Henderson. "I know the deputy doesn't see a connection to Helena, but nothing else makes sense." She rubbed her forehead. "There's been no ransom demand for her return. Do you think she's been trafficked?"

The thought of his beautiful sister in the hands of a human trafficker sickened him. "I thought of that when she first went missing, but could find no evidence she had been nabbed by any of the active rings in New York."

"What about drugs?"

Henderson winced. "I know she took them. I could tell she was desperate for a fix the last time I saw her, although she denied it. I didn't see any needle marks either."

"Not all drugs are injected by needles," Elle said.

"I know that." He had seen many a drug addict during his time as a public defender and as a prosecutor. "Her teeth looked okay, so I don't think she was taking meth either."

"Anything else about her physical appearance?"

"Her skin had a sallow tint and her short, sleeveless dress had hung on her much-too-thin frame." He swallowed hard to dislodge the emotion at remembering how awful she'd looked. "Her once thick, shiny hair had been pulled back into a messy ponytail that did little to hide its greasy sheen."

"Maybe it's not drugs." Elle stifled a yawn as Alec returned to the kitchen.

"The fire marshal said everything's okay in the backyard, and a deputy will remain on duty outside for the rest of the night," Alec said. "I suggest we all try to get a little shuteye now that the excitement has died down."

"I'm so sorry this is happening…" Henderson began, guilt rising over bringing trouble to Tall Trees.

The Stratmans exchanged a glance. "We have

a little experience with this sort of thing," Alec said. "Now they've made it personal—whoever they are—by trying to burn down our house."

Isabella linked her arm through Alec's. "Which was a big mistake on their part. Alec is like a bloodhound when it comes to sniffing out danger."

"A bloodhound, am I?" Alec squeezed his wife's waist. "Whatever I am, we'll talk more tomorrow—I mean later today—and see if we can't figure out a game plan."

"Sounds good." Elle yawned. "I can't believe I'm even the least bit tired."

"It's the chamomile tea, which has been used for years as a homeopathic sleep aid," Isabella said as she bid Elle and Henderson good-night.

Henderson mounted the stairs behind Elle, his steps dragging as the night's events caught up with him. They parted at the top of the stairs with a tentative plan to have brunch or lunch together to catch up, then he tumbled into bed after removing only his shoes. His last thought before sleep claimed him was of Elle—and how hard it would be to tell her he couldn't pursue a relationship with her. Seeing his mother looking so frail in the hospital bed had strengthened his resolve to find Helena as soon as possible. To do so, he needed to have his thoughts off an attractive podcaster and fully focused on chasing down every lead, no matter how slim. He would grant his mother's dearest wish to see her daughter alive again even if it meant destroying his own chance at happiness.

Elle applied sunscreen to the back of her neck. With her hair in a ponytail, she didn't want the skin to burn in the warm sunshine. Henderson had texted her, asking to meet him out back for an al fresco lunch. The chamomile tea had helped lull her back to sleep, and she'd awakened after noon feeling more rested than she'd expected.

In the kitchen, she greeted Isabella, who was arranging plates, napkins and silverware into a wicker basket. "Good afternoon."

"Did you manage to sleep after the night's events?" Isabella added a glass bottle of home-made lemonade.

"Yes, the tea must have done the trick." Elle grabbed two of the wrapped peaches from the mesh bag. "Is the basket for us?"

Isabella nodded. "I'll carry it outside if you want to wash those peaches."

Elle agreed and unwrapped the fruit. As she did, a folded piece of paper fluttered to the floor. She washed the peaches, wrapped them in a paper towel to blot the excess water, then picked up the paper.

Isabella entered the kitchen. "Henderson's waiting for you."

Elle stuffed the paper into her pocket before

carrying the peaches out back. Henderson stood near the blackened circles. She put the peaches on the wrought-iron table and walked over. "Good thing you arrived home when you did."

He circled the area. "And that Alec woke up when he did. I was only armed with my phone, which might not have been enough to stop their intention to firebomb the house."

She gazed at the grand old home. "Isabella told me Alec's great-aunt left the house to them a couple of years ago." She slanted a look at Henderson. "She said it was the aunt's way of match-making, since they weren't married at the time."

"Elle, I have something to tell you."

His serious tone sent her heart thumping in her chest. When he didn't say anything else, she prompted, "I'm listening."

"I've enjoyed spending time with you."

Elle dropped her eyes to the grass at the familiar refrain. How many times had she heard that from a man she'd thought was interested in her? Her mother was right—she was hopeless when it came to keeping a man.

"I think the world of you but I, we—" He stopped, blowing out a breath.

She waited like a prisoner on the gallows for the death blow. When he didn't continue, she jerked her head up, her eyes colliding with his. Ignoring the misery in their brown depths, she challenged him. "Spit it out."

"It's not you." He ran a hand over his beard. "My mom's had a heart attack—she's having surgery right now to fix a blocked artery."

The news stunned Elle, momentarily distracting her from her own heartache. "I thought it wasn't serious."

"She had another heart attack, a bad one, after I'd left yesterday. My aunt is with her, and my mom insisted that I stay here and find Helena. All she wants is to see her daughter again." His eyes pleaded for understanding. "I can't afford to be distracted from my mission."

The words doused the hope that he was interested in her as a woman, not as a means to find his sister. "So all I am is a distraction to you?"

"I didn't say that."

She waited for him to clarify, her arms crossed tightly at her chest as if to hold in her aching heart. The silence stretched out between them like a vast gorge she had no idea how to cross. When she couldn't stand it another second, she blurted, "And kissing me was just a distraction as well?"

Henderson flinched but didn't rush to correct her assumption.

"I see." Blinking rapidly to stave off the avalanche of tears threatening to break, she turned on her heel and marched to the back door. With each step, hope that he'd call her back died a little bit more. At the door, she drew in a breath.

Only the twittering of birds behind her. No footfalls. No other sound. Hot tears spilled down her cheeks. Her head high, she yanked open the door. Once in the house, she stood stock-still for a split second before dashing up the stairs.

Henderson forced himself to let Elle go, telling himself over and over it was for the best. He had to concentrate solely on tracking down Helena. They were so close—he could feel it in his bones. Time might be running out for his mom, and he had to bring Helena home before that happened. He couldn't fail now.

The hurt and bewilderment in Elle's expressive eyes tore at his heart. He hadn't meant to devastate her, convincing himself he was the one with a heart at risk, not her. That their kiss had meant more to him than it had to her. But her words, her reaction, revealed that for the lie it was. The urge to go to her, to apologize for his callous words, rose up in his throat, but he couldn't utter them. Not now.

"Did Elle forget something?" Isabella wore a straw hat and gardening gloves, a basket with tools looped over one arm.

"No, she, uh, something came up," he finished lamely.

"I see." Isabella threw him a look that made him squirm then, with a wave, she proceeded to the back corner where a flower bed bordered the neighbor's yard.

His appetite gone, Henderson nevertheless sat at the table and pulled food from the basket. Isabella had gone to a lot of trouble putting the picnic together, so he would try to at least sample the meal. He'd arranged everything when Alec sauntered from the house and dropped into the chair beside him.

"Elle's crying her eyes out in her room." Alec reached for a plate and loaded it up with chicken salad from a container. "You wouldn't happen to know anything about that, would you?"

Henderson hung his head, dishing up a miniscule spoonful of the salad. "I might."

Alec grunted. "You, my friend, have some explaining to do."

While the two men ate—Alec devouring his wife's chicken salad and Henderson only picking at his serving—Henderson updated Alec on the conversation. He sipped lemonade while Alec digested the details.

"It seems to me you made a rookie mistake." Alec placed one of the peaches on his plate and neatly sliced it off the pit.

"Okay, I'll bite." Henderson accepted a slice of peach. "What mistake?"

"First, you assumed that having a relationship with Elle would distract you from the search for your sister."

Henderson frowned as he chewed the fruit. "That's only logical. Multitasking is a myth."

Alec pointed the paring knife at Henderson. "Ah, but that's because you're not assessing the situation correctly."

"That's my second mistake?" Henderson ate another slice.

"Uh-huh." Alec finished the first peach and went on to the second. "Tell me something. How much mental energy were you expending trying not to be attracted to Elle?"

The question rocked Henderson. "Quite a lot, if I'm being honest."

"And how much less energy would you expend if you both admitted to your mutual attraction?"

Absently eating more of the peach slices put on his plate by Alec, he mulled the question. If he stopped fighting his growing feelings for Elle and instead embraced them, they would probably work better together without the undercurrent of uncertainty coloring every interaction. "Probably more than I realize."

"Exactly." Alec grinned as he brought out the final container. "My wife's brownies are the best—have one, and then we'll plan your strategy for getting your giant foot out of your mouth and winning back the fair Elle."

FIFTEEN

Elle splashed cold water on her face then assessed the damage her crying jag had inflicted. Puffy, red-rimmed eyes stared back at her from the bathroom mirror. "Stupid girl," she told her reflection. "When will you learn?"

Her mother's voice, pointing out Elle's feminine defaults, rattled around her mind. Born late in life to a wealthy couple more interested in themselves than in a child, Elle had been left mostly to her own devices with a series of nannies. Her jet-setting parents had popped in and out of her childhood like exotic creatures. When Elle had gone against her parents' wishes to study journalism instead of the law or politics, her father had nearly disowned her. Despite the success of *Gone Without a Trace*, her father kept asking when she would "put aside all this podcasting nonsense" and get a "real" job. Better than her mother, who doled out dating tips Elle neither asked for nor wanted to follow.

Breathing deeply, she smoothed her skirt over her hips. Something crinkled in her pocket, and she pulled out the piece of paper that had been with the peaches. Unfolding it, she studied the series of lines, with no words, on the page. Rotating it ninety degrees brought no clarity to what she was seeing. At a hundred and eighty degrees, the meaning of the lines suddenly made sense—she was looking at a map with tiny details.

Using her phone's magnifier app, she deciphered a cornfield to the right of the line she assumed was a road with a mailbox shaped like a tractor halfway down. She'd seen that mailbox— the Grays had one at the end of their driveway. Her nerves tingled as she oriented the map using the Gray house as a marker. Past the Gray house, a tiny squiggle appeared to indicate an entrance. Halfway up that drive, a small *X* marked a spot underneath a tree with a low fork splitting the trunk in half. The magnifier picked up a faint number 12 etched into the tree trunk. Possibilities raced through her mind. The little girl's wide eyes and timid smile. The way she'd carefully wrapped her peaches. Hazel must have slipped this note in with the fruit.

But who was she? And did the 12 mean come at midnight? If it had been last night, she had missed it.

Her stomach growled, reminding her of the missed lunch with Henderson. Fresh tears threat-

ened, but she refused to shed any more over what
might have been. Time to focus on solving Helena's disappearance and putting together the next
season of *Gone*.

Her phone buzzed. A text from Sabina.

Found your mysterious compound! Followed your
advice re Buffalo news articles about Obadiah
Judd. Sent you deets in email. Exciting!

Elle's tummy rumbled again. Crossing to the
window, she noted Henderson's SUV sat in the
parking lot. With stealth, she could slip out the
front and nip down to the café for a late lunch and
read Sabina's email. Then she could decide if she
would attempt to find the tree tonight in the hope
that whoever had sent the note would be there.

Tiptoeing down the stairs, she made it out of
the B and B without encountering anyone. She
walked quickly down the drive to avoid running
into Henderson or the Stratmans. She did not
want to explain the remnants of her tears to Alec
or Isabella.

Twenty minutes later, Elle set aside her empty
bowl of broccoli-cheddar soup and opened her
laptop to pull up Google maps to compare it with
the hand-drawn one. Much too far to walk. She'd
need to get a rental car, since the body shop had
informed her yesterday that her vehicle had been
totaled. One rental company would allow her to

fill out the paperwork online and would bring the vehicle to her. She scheduled delivery at the B and B for 4:00 p.m.

Sorting through her email, she found the one from Sabina.

Hey, Elle. On a hunch, I traced Obadiah Judd from New York to Virginia. He sold the New York property ten years ago and purchased the Dermott farm near Jayho Hollow, about 10 miles from Twin Oaks. His ownership is hidden under several layers of dummy corporations, but it was no match for my sleuthing skills. Both Obadiah and wife, Nalani, are listed as joint owners.

Judd operated a cash-only landscaping company in New York called Sonshine Landscaping. I only found it through a complaint on the Better Business Bureau website, as the business wasn't ever registered in the state. They call their Virginia place "Sonshine Co-op." He's attracted some followers who like his brand of Christianese coupled with some sort of utopia community with people living off the land. His central message is about love and getting back to nature. The compound—which is what some outsiders have called it—has its own electricity powered by solar panels and separate septic system, along with a well for fresh water. The Judds' latest tax return shows their income at a modest $50,000, mostly derived from their booth at farmers markets and local festivals.

There were some rumors I couldn't substantiate about Obadiah dabbling in a various grassroots organization, but there have been no run-ins with local law enforcement. But then I added the snake tattoo and found a whole lot more. The symbol has been adopted by a group calling themselves the Copperheads. It was difficult to find exactly what the Copperheads believe, but below are links to articles about the group's activities in other states.

Be careful! Sabina

Elle skimmed the articles, which portrayed the Copperheads as a biker gang in West Virginia, pro-marijuana proponents in Colorado, and neo-Nazis in Alabama. Some Copperheads staged protests at local and state government buildings in favor of the legalization of pot. While the various groups all used the Copperheads designation, it appeared each was a separate entity.

Sonshine Co-op's website said nothing about the Copperheads, and simply listed farmers markets and festivals where the co-op would have a booth, and the things it sold. Besides produce, the group sold handmade quilts, old-fashioned wooden toys, and Christmas ornaments. Quite an eclectic mix of merchandise. No address was listed and a webform was the only way to contact the group. Sonshine Co-op's social media accounts were filled with stylized photos of its merchandise and memes of inspirational quotes about the joys of the simple life.

Elle flagged the waitress down for a refill of iced tea then spent the next few hours outlining the first three episodes of the podcast. After sending the outline and the recording of her car interview with Henderson to Caren, she paid her bill, adding a generous tip for monopolizing a table for so long.

On her walk back to Tall Trees, Caren called.

"Great outline. I haven't listened to the recording yet."

"Thanks."

"Goodness, your voice has become quite husky. How's your throat?"

"Sore. The doctor prescribed a throat spray that's helping with the pain." Elle detoured to sit on a bench under the shade of a large tree in the town's park. "I wasn't expecting you to reply until tomorrow since it's Sunday."

"Tyrone took the kids to visit his mom for the day, and you know how much my mother-in-law loves and admires me."

Elle laughed. "From what you've told me, she's not all bad. I think you enjoy having time by yourself sometimes and that's why you encourage your husband to go without you."

"If that were true, you'd think I would have better plans than catching up on my work email. Since that's not the case, let's discuss where you're at in the hunt for Helena." Caren paused. "Which is going to be my suggestion for the season's title."

"'Hunting for Helena'?" Elle rolled the words around in her head as a possibility. "It's alliterate, which I know you like."

"It's catchy too, and different enough from the first two titles."

Elle agreed. *Gone Without a Trace*'s first season had been titled "Searching for Sara" and its second, "Finding Frank."

"Let's talk about audio. What other interviews have you done?"

Time to confess. "I've only done the Henderson one." She hurried on before Caren could chide her. "But I did record my conversation with Kathleen when she called about Helena's phone call."

"Good. Send me that," her editor directed. "Who else will you interview?"

Elle ticked off the short list of names. "Tomorrow afternoon, I have an interview scheduled with the sheriff's office press liaison—couldn't get the sheriff or deputy to agree to an interview—and on Tuesday morning with the editor of the *Twin Oaks Gazette* for background on the town. I figured we could edit out my scratchy voice as needed and I can rerecord anything when my voice is back to normal. Have you read what Sabina found about Obadiah Judd and the Sonshine Co-op?"

"Yes, but I don't see the connection to Helena Parker."

"There's a slim thread—Henderson thinks the van that picked up Helena from the courthouse the last time he physically laid eyes on her had the words 'Sonshine Landscaping' on the side," Elle explained. "It's too much of a coincidence in my book that Sonshine Co-op is now operating some sort of hippie utopia in the same area where Henderson spotted Helena in the parade photo."

"As long as you don't get distracted from the main objective, take a look into Sonshine Co-op, but be careful. This Copperheads group seems fringy, which can mean people involved aren't thinking straight."

"I'm always careful."

"The other two cases didn't have people shooting at you or trying to burn down the house where you're staying," Caren reminded her. "I'd hate to lose my best podcast journalist."

"I won't take any unnecessary risks." Elle silenced the voice whispering she planned to do just that with her midnight foray to *X* marks the spot on the map.

"Promise me you won't go off by yourself—

that someone *local* will know your whereabouts."
Caren sighed. "I mean it, Elle."

The friendship in Caren's voice warmed her
heart. "I know, and I promise."

Elle disconnected, tapping the phone against
her leg as her conscious twinged. She would be
very careful, but perhaps she should heed Caren's
advice and let someone know her whereabouts.
She drew the line at telling Henderson—she was
a means to an end with him, and she would not
give him the chance to hurt her again.

Henderson slapped at a mosquito, irritated he
hadn't taken Isabella up on her offer of bug spray
before he'd left for a walk in the woods. Twin
Oaks had developed thirty miles of trails circling
the town and through the surrounding woods
southwest of Main Street. On a warm Sunday
afternoon, a good many people walked, biked
and ran on the paved path.

While he tried to keep his thoughts focused
on the little progress they'd made to find his sister, Elle's stricken face refused to leave his mind.
How could he have been so callous in telling her
he couldn't have a relationship at this time? He
should have said he found her immensely attractive but he owed his mother his undivided attention to search for Helena. That the guilt he felt
for not looking harder when his sister first lost
contact with the family weighed him down like

Marley's chains in *A Christmas Carol*. That the fading hope in his mother's eyes tore at his heart. That the last words his father had spoken to him had been to extract a promise from Henderson to bring Helena home.

He swatted another mosquito away. Maybe if he'd told Elle that instead of letting her assume he didn't view her as girlfriend material, she would have understood. Alec's words replayed in his mind. "How much mental energy were you expending trying not to be attracted to Elle?"

Too much even before their kiss. His lips tingled with the memory of her soft mouth. This would not do at all.

The path wound past a playground where a group of kids tumbled over the equipment. Happy laughter filled the air, along with squeals and shouts, as the children played. Longing for a family of his own stabbed his chest. He had thought himself not able to love, but his time with Elle had proved that to not be the case.

Now he found himself on the brink of falling in love with a beautiful woman but having to push her away to fulfill his obligation to his family. His father's words, spoken when he'd turned thirteen, returned to his mind. "Son, you're growing into a man as your sister is growing into a woman. As the older sibling, it's your responsibility to keep your sister from harm."

And he'd tried. Lord knew, he'd tried. His

father hadn't always seen that, often blaming Henderson for Helena's increasingly dangerous escapades. The weight of his sister's disappearance pressed down on him, squeezing his chest. *Lord, help me to stop thinking about Elle. Help me to focus on finding my sister. Help my mom recover from surgery without complications.*

Lengthening his stride, he pumped his arms. If he hadn't been recovering from a shin fracture, he would have laced up his running shoes and run away from his problems. A brisk walk would have to do. Fishing his earbuds out of his pocket, he inserted them before cranking up some heavy metal music. If ever he needed some head-banging tunes, it was today.

Ninety minutes and seven miles later, Henderson entered the B and B, wiping sweat from his brow. The walk had cleared his pores, but it hadn't cleared his head. Thoughts of Elle still dominated. Maybe he could make it up to her by taking her to a nice dinner and explaining more fully his decision to not pursue a relationship. Four thirty-five. He paused outside her door, but a glance at his sweaty body made him scurry into his own room. Shower first, then an apology followed by a dinner invitation.

Two hours later, he knocked at her door. His aunt's call with an update on his mother's condition had delayed his shower. Thankfully, the surgery had gone well and she was resting. The doctors said Kathleen would stay until at least Wednesday. His mom, groggy from the remnants of the anesthesia, hadn't spoken with him long. But hearing her voice had renewed his sense of urgency in finding Helena—and solidified the rightness of his resolve to put his growing feelings for Elle on hold until he did.

Then a contact in the FBI who specialized in gang-related tattoos had responded to his query about the snake Milly had sketched with the news it represented the Copperheads, a grassroots group with cells around the country.

They're not organized enough for any large-scale effort but the FBI has them on our watch list. We suspect they're behind some bombings and protests.

Henderson had responded with what info they had on a potential cell near Twin Oaks, Virginia.

Elle still hadn't answered his knock. He knocked again. Harder.

"She's out," Isabella said from the top of the stairs. "Not sure when she'll be back."

"Ah, thanks."

Henderson decided to walk into town for a quick bite to eat then returned and waited for Elle in the living room off the front door with his Roosevelt biography. He'd tamped down disappointment in missing her, but consoled himself that as soon as he found Helena, he could turn his thoughts to the pretty podcaster.

A thump jerked Henderson awake. Beyond the glow of the lamp, the rest of the room lay in shadows. His book lay on the floor beside his chair. Nearly midnight. He must have dozed off. The last check of the time had been around ten thirty, but Elle still hadn't returned to the B and B. Perhaps she'd snuck by him while he'd slept. Stretching, he collected his book, turned off the light, and made his way upstairs guided by the dimmed hall lights.

He pressed his ear to her door but heard nothing through the thick oak. Softly, he knocked. Nothing. He rapped harder. Still nothing. He tried her phone but it rolled straight to voicemail, indicating she probably had it silenced. Maybe she'd answer a text.

Hey, Elle. Need to talk. You okay?

Depositing his book on the bedside table in his room, he paced, refreshing the screen on his phone every couple of seconds to see if Elle had responded to his text. After ten minutes with no answer, he hustled downstairs to see if a new rental car was in the lot. Isabella had said Elle had gotten one that very afternoon. Only his SUV and the Tall Trees Land Rover occupied spaces.

Unease slithered up his spine. Where was Elle?

He had ignored the many times his instinct had pushed him to confront Helena about her activities and lived to regret it. He wouldn't make the same mistake with someone he cared about—and he admitted to himself he cared about Elle very much. Sending Alec a text asking him to come downstairs, he paced until the innkeeper joined him.

"Where's Elle?" Henderson didn't bother to explain his concern. The other man could surely see it on his face.

Alec frowned. "She's not in her room?"

"If she is, she didn't answer my knocks, and she's not answering her phone—call or texts." Henderson gripped his phone. "I'm concerned." Henderson pointed to the front door. "Her car isn't in the lot either."

"Let's check her room." Alec turned on his heel and headed for the stairs. Henderson followed. With a master key, Alec unlocked her door, flipping the switch to bathe the room in light.

A quick sweep told Henderson that Elle wasn't in residence.

Alec had his phone out. "Let me check with Isabella."

Henderson prowled the room, anxiety clawing at him with every turn. It was his fault Elle had gone off on her own. If he hadn't pushed her away with his clumsy attempt at self-preservation, she would have told him her intentions.

"You need to hear this," Alec said, thrusting his phone at Henderson.

"Isabella?"

"I'm sorry. I didn't see the note until Alec called me." The panic in her voice sent his own pulse into orbit.

"What note?" Henderson barely kept his voice even when every nerve wanted to scream.

"This one," Isabella said as she entered Elle's room.

Henderson gave the phone back to Alec and reached for the folded piece of paper.

"She must have slipped it under our door, but I didn't notice and probably kicked it under the side table next to the entrance," Isabella babbled, distress evident in every line of her face.

Henderson unfolded it, finding a second piece of paper tucked inside a drawing. He started with the note.

Isabella & Alec,
I'm off on what's probably a wild-goose chase, but I promised my editor I wouldn't go without telling somebody. And, to be honest, I didn't text or phone because I knew you would probably tell me not to go or insist on coming with me.

I received the enclosed drawing with my peaches. I think the little girl put it there when she wrapped the fruit. I'm hoping she'll be there at midnight tonight, even though she gave me the note yesterday. I'll wait an hour then head back to Tall Trees. Elle

Henderson crumpled the note in his hand. It was already ten till midnight. "Where is this?"

Alec traced the lines, turning the map this way and that before settling on an orientation. "This appears to be the Gray farm, so this must be an entrance past their driveway."

"It's part of the old Dermott farm property?" Where they'd seen the man with the snake tattoo.

"I believe so," Alec responded. "What else is going on?"

Henderson relayed what his FBI contact had said about the Copperheads. "If they are part of that group, Elle could be in even more danger. I'm going to find her."

SIXTEEN

Elle crouched down, glad she'd bought dark stretch pants and a thin, black, long-sleeved shirt at Walmart before going to her stakeout. A black lightweight scarf hid her hair and a liberal dose of bug spray kept most of the insects away. She shifted, wishing she'd remembered to grab her water bottle from the car. She'd parked on the verge of the Gray's driveway, backing up as much as possible into a clump of bushes to hide the vehicle.

Shielding her phone, she checked the time. Twelve fifteen. From her vantage point across the narrow lane, the tree with the V-shaped trunks stood near the road. Her excitement about a possible break in the case had ebbed with each passing minute. Why hadn't she eaten a peach yesterday? Or at least unwrapped them all? The delay had probably cost her finding out why Hazel had wanted to see her in the first place.

Twelve twenty. She'd give it ten more minutes.

A small figure darted out of the woods on the other side.

Elle held her breath as moonlight reflected off a pair of glasses. Hazel reached the tree, standing on tiptoes to put her hand in the base of the *V.* She pulled something out, glanced around, then put it back into the tree.

Elle started to rise when the hairs on the back of her neck prickled, telling her to stay hidden.

Hazel moved away, hugging the tree line parallel with the dirt road. Headlights sliced through the darkness, illuminating Hazel, who froze.

Elle shrank back into the brambles as the vehicle stopped. A man disembarked, a rifle slung over his shoulder with a strap.

"Hey, what are you doing out there at this time of night?" Recognition sliced through Elle at the man's voice. It was the driver who'd told her to leave the property.

"I couldn't sleep," Hazel replied as her body trembled.

The man grabbed her arm, shaking the girl violently. "You know better. No one leaves their building at lockdown."

"I'm sorry!" Hazel began to sob. "I didn't mean to—"

"The commander will deal with you in the morning." The man dragged her to the Jeep and shoved her inside before joining her. "Let's go."

The Jeep made a tight turn then rumbled away.

Elle waited five minutes to make sure they wouldn't suddenly double back, then darted across the road to the tree. Thrusting her hand inside the *V*, which had created a hollow inside the trunk, she grabbed a plastic zip-topped bag. Not bothering to look, she tucked it into the waistband of her pants at the small of her back, pulling her shirt over it.

Another quick glance down the road showed no movement or vehicles. Time to get out of there. Saying a prayer for Hazel's safety, she walked rapidly toward the main road, keeping as close to the trees and bushes as possible. The moon broke through the clouds, giving her enough light to see the cross street ahead.

Elle picked up her pace but something snagged her foot, sending her sprawling to the ground. At the same time, the sound of dogs barking rent the night air. She caught her breath, easing slowly to her feet as a male voice shouted something she couldn't distinguish. Turning her head to see the lane behind her, Elle bit back a scream at the sight of two armed men each holding dogs straining at their leashes. The men halted by the tree where Hazel had hidden the package, the dogs sniffing around the base.

As quietly as possible, Elle stepped deeper into the trees and moved as rapidly as doable toward the main road. Her stomach churned at the thought of the dogs coming after her. Her father loved big dogs; he'd owned a pair of Chesapeake Bay retrievers that had terrified Elle as a child. Memories of being chased by the large, exuberant canines pushed her fear even higher and she stumbled again, going to her hands and knees.

Pain shot through her palms as something sharp pierced the skin. Scrambling to her feet, she broke into a jog. A hundred yards ahead, the cross road beckoned.

The baying sound of dogs on the hunt spurred her into a full-out run. Fifty yards to go. The barking grew louder. With a half sob, she pushed herself harder. A man shouted behind her but she didn't turn her head.

Bursting through the trees, she tumbled into the drainage ditch at the side of the road. Clawing her way out on her hands and knees, she gained her feet and broke into a run. Half a mile to safety. Surely, the men wouldn't pursue her on a county road. But the dogs—now freed from their leashes—rounded the corner and soon caught up with her. Both nipped at her heels, their growls low and vicious. Something held them back from outright attacking her, of that she was certain. The animals toyed with her, easily keeping pace and snapping their jaws from time to time.

Up ahead, she spied the outline of her car. She could do it. She could make it. Her key fob. Where was her key fob? She pressed the pocket of her pants, relief flooding her senses as her fingers brushed over the object.

Putting on a burst of speed, she pressed what she hoped was the unlock button through the fabric of her pants' pocket. Lights flashed on her vehicle. Beyond her car, headlights roared toward her. Fear clawed at her throat. They had her surrounded. Clouds covered the moon, plunging the road into near darkness. She hit the unlock button on the fob to activate the lights again to orient her. Nearly there. Then one of the dogs cut sharply in front of her, sending her tumbling to the ground.

Henderson stomped his foot on the mat in the passenger side of Alec's Land Rover as the SUV sped through the night toward the Gray farm—and Elle. While he knew Alec would make better time, given the other man's familiarity with the roads, the urgency roiling through his body needed an outlet.

"Nearly there."

The assurance did little to calm Henderson's nerves. "I have a bad feeling about this."

Alec didn't answer, but the vehicle leaped forward as if the man had accelerated even more. He braked slightly to take a turn. The headlights illuminated inky blackness as the moon slid behind the clouds. The sound of barking dogs penetrated the inside of the SUV, ratcheting up Henderson's fear.

"Do you hear that?" Henderson leaned forward, straining to see beyond the headlights. He powered down his window as someone cried out. "I think that's Elle!"

Alec braked hard as a figure fell to the ground, the dogs circling and growling. Throwing the SUV into Park, he grabbed the shotgun from the rack above the bench seat while Henderson launched himself out of the vehicle, not bothering to close the door behind him.

"Elle!" Henderson raced to her as she lay still in a pool of light from the headlights on the ground. The dogs circled her, growling. When Henderson got within a few feet, one turned and bared its teeth in his direction. He froze.

Beside him, Alec racked a bullet and raised his gun, aiming straight at the dog. "If you don't want your dog shot, I suggest you call both of them back now."

Standing several feet behind the dogs, Henderson could now see two men, rifles held in their hands. For one horrible moment, neither moved, then one of the men whistled. The dog pricked up its ears, although its attention didn't waver from Henderson. Another whistle and the dog whirled and bounded toward the men, its companion following.

Henderson dropped to his knees beside Elle, who pushed herself to a seated position. "Are you okay?"

"I think so." She held out shaking hands in front of her. "Maybe not. I was so scared." A tear slipped down her cheek.

Henderson cupped her face, using his thumb to wipe away the tear trail. "You weren't the only one."

"We'd better get going," Alec said.

Henderson rose and helped Elle to her feet. She staggered against him, and he slid his arm around her waist, hugging her body to his. "I'll drive Elle's car."

"Good idea." Alec didn't lower his weapon. "I'll stand guard until you get safely inside."

Henderson nodded then guided Elle to her vehicle. His hands shook as he closed the door and walked around the hood to the driver's side. Too close. If he and Alec hadn't arrived in time…

Elle huddled in her seat on the drive back to Tall Trees. Henderson held off questioning her about the night's events, allowing her privacy to regain her composure. Once at the B and B, Alec led the way into the cheery kitchen, plugging in the electric kettle.

"Tea and then talk," he said as he arranged

mugs and an assortment of tea bags. "My English grandmother always said a nice cup of tea soothed the soul."

"She sounds like a wise woman." Elle selected decaf Darjeeling, her hands shaking a little as she placed the bag in a mug.

"She was," Alec said.

"Do I have time to change?" Elle gestured at her all-black outfit, bits of debris and damp smears of what might have been dog saliva clinging to the fabric.

"Of course, and if you want to take a quick shower, I can easily reheat the water for your cup when you come back down," Alec said.

"Thanks." Elle left.

Henderson watched her until she exited the kitchen. She didn't move like she'd sustained any injuries she hadn't told him about, which eased his mind a little.

"That was a close call," Alec said as he poured steaming water over the tea bags in two of the mugs.

"Much too close. I think I've aged a decade." Henderson tugged his mug closer to him, breathing in the scent of peppermint, one of his favorite herbal teas. Helena had become interested in tea as a young teenager, reading up on the different health properties of black, white, green, oolong, and herbal varieties. He hadn't paid much attention but hadn't been able to escape endless tea tastings. Many he hadn't liked, but peppermint continued to be a late-night favorite.

"That's what being in love will do to you."

Henderson gaped at Alec, who merely smirked. "Love? I barely know the woman."

"It doesn't take a psychologist to see you two are crazy about each other—but neither one of you wants to admit it outright." Alec took out his teabag, laying it on a tea coaster in the shape of a teapot. "Even I could see the attraction zinging between you and Elle."

Henderson added his teabag to the coaster. "I like her. But love? I don't think I'm ready for something like that. Not with Helena still missing and my mom in the hospital." His chest constricted at his mother's last words to him about finding his sister.

Alec laid a hand on Henderson's shoulder. "Like we discussed earlier, don't let your quest squeeze out a chance at love."

"I will take it under advisement." Elle's pale face and large eyes filled his mind. She hadn't broken through his defenses—she'd slipped around them without him even knowing, finding her way to his heart.

"I decided I needed a quick shower to wash away the stench of those animals," Elle said when she reentered the kitchen.

Henderson admired her long legs in a pair of jean capris and her soft yellow T-shirt. Her bare feet padded softly on the hardwood floor.

"Let me warm up your water." Alec busied himself with the electric kettle, turning his back on Henderson and Elle.

"Feeling better?" Henderson stepped closer to Elle.

"I think my pulse is back in the normal range." She blew out a breath. "But I don't mind admitting how terrified I was—or how grateful that you two came along when you did."

Henderson gave in to his impulse and gathered her to him in what he intended to be a loose hug. When her arms circled his waist, his own tightened, drawing her closer. Her head fell against his chest. He stroked her back, burrowing his face in her hair to breathe in the sweet floral scent he'd come to associate with Elle.

The beeping of the electric kettle broke the moment and Elle stepped out of his embrace. "Thank you. I needed that."

Her quiet admission made him want to drop a kiss on her lips, but Alec's presence kept him from acting on the impulse. Maybe he would follow the innkeeper's advice and tell Elle how he felt. But for now, learning exactly what Elle had found out during her midnight adventure took top priority.

Once Elle had doctored her tea with sugar and a healthy dose of cream, they all settled at the table. She cupped her hands around the mug then sighed. "I suppose you want to know what happened."

Alec and Henderson exchanged a look, but neither answered.

"If you found the map and note—which I assume you did, since you arrived in the nick of time—then you know why I was there." Elle took a sip of her tea before telling them her movements from the time she'd arrived until their rescue. She reached behind her and drew out the plastic bag. "Shall we see what Hazel left for us to find?"

"Wait a minute. We should document this before opening it." Alec drew out his phone and snapped several photos of the bag, which appeared to hold folded pieces of paper. He then went to a drawer and brought a box of latex gloves to the table. "We'd better put these on as well."

"Good thinking." Usually, Henderson would have thought of preserving potential evidence, but finding Elle surrounded by growling dogs had shaken him more than he cared to admit.

Once everyone had gloves, Elle reached inside the bag and drew out the packet of papers. Unfolding them, she scanned the first one. "It's a list of names." She handed it to Henderson.

Roughly sixty names were printed in double rows in alphabetical order by last name. Several names had a checkmark by them. Skimming down the page, he stopped when he came to Rose McCellan with a checkmark. Her husband, Hank, was listed above her name, but without a checkmark. He passed the paper to Alec. "I only recognize Rose McCellan's name. She's the one who died and her husband came to the clinic with a gun."

Alec ran his gloved finger down the list. "Let me check." He tapped something into his phone and waited, his brows knitting together. "The *Twin Oaks Gazette* ran a story last week about all the deaths related to meth. At the end, they ran obituaries of the six men and women." He looked up from his phone. "All six are on this list with checkmarks."

Henderson collated the information as if prepping for a case. "A logical deduction would be the names on this list are drug users, maybe even customers."

Alec nodded while Elle examined the other papers in the packet. "If that's true, then whoever made this list knew they were customers."

Henderson fit more pieces together. "What if they were tracking the users because it was a new batch of meth? Didn't Deputy Stubbs say something about a new source of meth flooding the county?"

"He did say something about that," Elle said. "But I'm not sure how that ties into Helena's disappearance."

"I don't either." Henderson slumped in his chair. "We can follow up on the names tomorrow, when our brains are fresher. What else was in the package?"

"It appears to be another map." Elle spread out the remaining four sheets, arranging them so that they formed one block. "I think I've oriented these right. There's nothing to indicate which piece goes where."

Henderson bent over the papers, immediately agreeing with Elle's assessment. The sketch was indeed a map. "There's the tree and lane." He traced his finger along the lane as it halted at a gate about a half mile further down from the tree where Hazel had left the packet. "It must be of the compound itself."

Alec tapped the far left corner. "This borders Appleby's Orchards. I'll call Bill Appleby in the morning and ask him about Sonshine Co-op as neighbors."

"His name really is Appleby?" Elle asked, a smile tugging at the corners of her mouth for the first time that night.

"Yeah, funny, huh? His family has owned that land for generations, with one of his greats planting the first apple orchard. Now they have a dozen varieties," Alec said.

They all shared a smile at the thought of apple farmers with a last name of Appleby, then Henderson returned his attention to the map. "There's quite a few buildings on the property. Alec, can you tell which are new and which might be holdovers from when Dermott farmed it?"

The innkeeper tapped a larger structure to the left of the tree lane. "This might be the old two-story farmhouse, which would mean these structures here and here are probably the old barn and storage shed." He indicated the two buildings fairly close to the house. "To my knowledge, Dermott didn't have any other buildings on the property."

"What did he farm?" Henderson eyed the drawing, noting several large stands of trees around where he would have expected farmland.

"I checked around with some of the town old-timers to see who remembered the last Dermott to live on the land," Alec said. "He mostly grew corn and soybeans, I think, but an ancestor tried apples for a time, planting two separate orchards on the land. Didn't make it as apple farmers because they were notoriously tight with money, so didn't want to pay the going rate for migrant pickers come harvest time. They haven't kept up with the orchards for at least forty or fifty years."

"That would be more than enough time to create mini forests in the old fruit groves," Elle said. "But I think we have an even bigger problem than overgrown apple orchards."

Henderson locked eyes with her, the serious expression in hers telling him he wasn't going to like what she was about to say.

"Look at this." She placed her finger on a building tucked on the far side of one of the apple groves.

Camouflaged in the shingles on the roof was a drawing of a copperhead snake.

SEVENTEEN

"That's the same snake as in the tattoo," Elle reminded the two men. "It appears there's a group of Copperheads right here in Twin Oaks."

"The FBI considers the group homegrown terrorists," Henderson added. "I heard back from an FBI friend about them, earlier today—" he glanced over in the direction of the kitchen wall clock "—make that yesterday. I was going to tell you but…"

"I vanished without a trace." Her allusion to the podcast eased a little of the tension building from her discovery. "Not sure this constitutes enough proof, but you should probably let your FBI contact know it appears a cell is operating nearby."

"I'll call him later today. Let me snap a photo of the building and map to send along." Henderson aimed his phone's camera at the drawing, snapping several photos. Then he stood on a chair to get the entire map within the frame. His sharp intake of breath made her shoulders tense.

"What is it?" She swept her eyes over the drawing, but nothing jumped out at her.

Still standing on the chair, he whispered, *"Vade ad victor spolia."*

"To the victor go the spoils?" Alec translated the Latin, his voice as puzzled as Elle felt.

Henderson pointed to the cluster of buildings that included the farmhouse. "On the roofs, she inserted the Latin phrase. *Vade ad* on the farmhouse, *victor* on the barn, and *spolia* on the shed."

Now that he pointed it out, Elle could see the words intertwined in the roof tiles, much like the reptile had been on the orchard building. Then the significance of his pronoun usage tickled her brain. "You said 'she.' Do you think Helena drew this map?"

Sinking back into his chair, Henderson nodded. "The summer we turned nine, our father hired a Latin tutor to teach us the language. Of course, being kids, we weren't thrilled to spend several hours a day during our summer vacation learning a dead language. But the tutor actually made it fun, teaching us pig Latin as well as noun declensions and vocabulary."

Elle detected a sheen of tears in his eyes at the memory. "Sounds like it wasn't all bad."

Henderson shrugged. "It wasn't, especially

the pig Latin. But it did give us one of our pet phrases."

"Vade ad victor spolia," Alec supplied.

"Exactly." Henderson flattened his palm on the map. "Helena drew this."

"And she used my encounter with Hazel to hand it off." Elle went through her meeting with the girl at the farmers market again in her mind. "What I don't understand is how Helena knew I would visit the co-op's booth."

"Maybe it was more a hope than a definite knowledge," Alec put in. "Isabella often takes B and B guests to the market."

"It wouldn't have been hard to find out where we were staying," Henderson said. "Especially since we suspect someone at Sonshine Co-op doesn't want us here."

"What we don't know is whether it's because of Helena or the Copperheads," Elle said. "We need to get on that compound and find out."

"That won't be easy," Henderson reminded her. "We know they keep a tight rein on who comes and goes. The main entrance has a gate with security cameras, and the back lane you were on appears to be regularly patrolled by men with dogs."

Elle shuddered. "I definitely don't want to get too close to those animals again, but surely they're kept in a kennel of some kind and wouldn't be roaming around unleashed."

"Probably not if there are kids on the grounds, as Hazel and Holden, the boy we found, live there," Henderson said.

Elle stifled a yawn. The adrenaline of the chase had faded completely, leaving her bone-tired.

"Let's call it a night and regroup in the morning," Alec said.

"Good idea." Henderson stacked the map and list of names together then slid them back into the plastic bag.

"Is tomorrow only Monday?" She stripped off her plastic gloves, adding them to Alec's and Henderson's in the middle of the table.

"Hard to believe, but yes," Henderson said. "Which reminds me—Deputy Stubbs asked us to come down to the sheriff's office and sign statements about the backyard incident."

"It seems all we do is sign statements." Elle pushed to her feet. "Should we tell him about what happened tonight?"

"I don't know." Henderson rose as well. "I'm not sure we can trust him."

"He's only been with the department for less than a year," Alec explained.

"We have to trust someone." Elle moved toward the door, the desire for sleep dragging her every step. "Maybe it should be him. Good night, Alec. Thanks again for helping me tonight."

"You're welcome. I hope you can sleep okay," Alec said.

Henderson echoed her good night and came alongside her as they headed for the stairs. "You sure you're okay? You look done in."

"What every girl wants to hear," she joked with a smile she didn't have the energy to hold for long. "I'm just exhausted. Running for your life with yipping dogs at your heels takes a lot out of you."

At the top of the stairs, she turned to Henderson. Foolish to hope he might kiss her, might have reconsidered his opinion of her. The way he'd held her after Alec chased off the dogs hadn't seemed indifferent. "But then you came to my rescue."

In the dim light of the hallway, she searched his eyes, but the shadows hid whatever emotions swam in their brown depths. When he didn't immediately answer, she sighed. "Good night."

Pivoting toward her room, she blinked hard at the sudden tears pricking her eyes. Remnants of the day's emotional roller coaster, that's all. Not tears over Henderson's rejection yet again.

"Elle, wait."

She froze, her back to him. Butterflies went bowling in her stomach, but she didn't dare turn around, not yet, not until he said something more. She didn't want him to see how vulnerable she was at that moment, on tenterhooks waiting to hear a word of admiration from his kissable lips.

"I'm so sorry about what I said to you earlier today—er, yesterday, I guess at this point. On the patio."

An apology, not a declaration of his feelings for her. She didn't answer right away, still holding out hope of more. When silence filled the space between them, Elle squared her shoulders. "It's okay," she told her door. "Don't worry—I won't misinterpret your offer of comfort tonight for anything more than a friendly gesture after a scary incident."

She slipped her key into the lock, opened the door and went inside without turning around to face Henderson. Once inside, she relocked the door, placing the key on a nearby table. Then she hurried to the bathroom, tears streaming down her cheeks.

Henderson trimmed his beard, concentrating on getting every wayward hair. Satisfied with the result, he replaced the trimmer on its charger and then finished his morning routine. Sleep had not come easy after his bungled attempt at an apology and confession with Elle. He'd nailed the apology apparently too well—convincing her he only regretted how he'd said what he'd said and not the subject of his words. His tongue, so agile in court, had been tied up in knots and he hadn't been able to untangle it quick enough to explain before she'd dashed into her room.

Maybe he'd have time to set things right before lunch. Alec had texted that since they were the only guests staying at Tall Trees for the moment, Isabella would be serving lunch instead of breakfast in the dining room starting at noon. His stomach reminded him food was of the essence. Telling his tummy to be quiet, he crept out of his room and across the hall as silently as possible to press his ear to Elle's door. Nothing. Maybe she'd already gone downstairs.

With a shrug, he descended and peeked into the dining room. Empty. A sweep of the first floor revealed no one. He stepped out the back door to take a look around the patio, but only the twitter of birds and the occasional squirrel greeted him.

Closing the door, he returned to the front hall, debating whether to knock on Elle's door, when the doorbell pealed. Since he was the closest to the entrance, he opened the door.

"I was in the area, so brought your statements," Deputy Stubbs said. "May I come in?"

"Of course," Henderson moved to allow the deputy to enter.

Stubbs handed him a folder. Henderson read over the statement and signed it. "Here you go."

"Good afternoon, Deputy," Isabella said from the dining room archway. "We were just about to sit down to lunch. Care to join us?"

Stubbs sniffed. "Is that your spinach and mushroom quiche I smell?"

"Why, yes it is," Isabella said.

"Then count me in." The deputy removed his hat, hanging it on one of a series of pegs on the wall near the door. "Mrs. Stratman makes the best spinach and mushroom quiche. I think it's the hint of nutmeg that elevates it to the realm of divine."

"I can't wait to taste this amazing dish," Henderson said as he followed the deputy into the dining room. "I didn't know you were such a connoisseur of quiche."

"My grandmother on my mother's side was a world-class pastry chef. Had her own shop for a time back home," Stubbs answered as he took the offered seat at one of the larger round tables.

Isabella laid an extra place setting to accommodate the deputy. "And where's home?"

"I grew up on out the outskirts of Cheyenne, Wyoming."

"You're a long way from Wyoming, Deputy," Henderson said as Isabella set a bowl of chicken salad on the table.

"That I am," Stubbs replied, his manner easy. But Henderson didn't miss the shrewd look in his eyes, as if knowing Henderson had more than pleasant conversation in mind.

"Good afternoon." Elle approached the table, looking pretty in a sundress with wide shoulder straps and some kind of cream-colored fabric over bright green material. The full skirt swished as she sat in the chair Alec held for her. "Thank you."

"Ms. Updike, would you please read and sign your statement?" Stubbs handed her another folder.

While Elle did so, Isabelle brought out a basket of rolls and a fruit salad. Elle scribbled her name on the statement and gave it back to the deputy.

"I think that's everything," Isabella said as she took a seat. "Alec, would you please say a blessing on our food?"

"Of course." Alec bowed his head and said a short prayer of thanks for their lunch. "Deputy, if you want to start the rolls around?"

Stubbs reached for the basket. "This all looks amazing, Mrs. Stratman."

"Thank you." Isabella smiled and passed the deputy a slice of quiche. Conversation centered around the food and the apple harvest currently underway in the valley. After their bellies were full, Isabella served coffee and homemade chocolate-chip cookies for dessert.

Stubbs bit into his cookie. "Mmm. I think these are the best chocolate-chip cookies I've ever eaten, Mrs. Stratman. I detect something unique in them, am I right?"

"It's an old family recipe my great-grandfather

developed back in Mexico, and yes, there is an unusual ingredient," Isabella said.

"And if you tell me, you'll have to kill me?" Stubbs took another cookie.

"Something like that," Isabella agreed.

Henderson sipped his coffee, wondering if Stubbs would get to the point of his visit so Henderson could talk privately with Elle. All through lunch, she had avoided him as much as possible. When their hands had brushed accidentally while passing the roll basket, she had actually flinched—not a good sign. Impatience swarmed around his gut like angry bees.

Just when he thought he would straight-up ask the deputy, Stubbs set down his empty cup, his expression turning serious. "Thank you again for lunch." Stubbs patted his flat midsection. "I don't know when I've had a more enjoyable meal, one I hate to ruin."

Henderson put down the sliver of cookie he'd been about to eat as the deputy made eye contact with Elle, Alec, then him.

"Our office received a complaint of trespassing against the three of you," Stubbs said. "Said Ms. Updike ventured on private property last night despite posted signs warning that trespassers would be prosecuted."

Henderson kept his expression neutral with effort. When he and Alec had come along, Elle had been in the middle of a public road. The bees in his stomach buzzed louder at the remembrance of how scared he'd been to see Elle on the pavement, two growling dogs snapping at her.

"And are you?" Elle asked, her voice cool and controlled.

"Am I what?" Stubbs said.

"Going to arrest me for trespassing." Elle opened a maps app on her phone, pinching to make the area larger. She turned the screen toward the deputy. "Because I'm pretty sure these are county roads, and as such, are open to the public."

Stubbs glanced at the map. "This one is." He pointed to the one that ran past the Gray farm. "But this lane is on private property." He indicated the one Elle had ventured down to find the tree.

"You would think so, since it bisects the old Dermott farm," Elle replied, something in her voice telling Henderson things might not be as they seemed. "But according to county records, it's actually County Road 4205 and goes straight through to County Road 4321 on the other side of the farm." She unfolded an area map, the roads in question highlighted in yellow. "I spent some time at the county surveyor's office this morning, and the nice clerk provided me with this map, marking the appropriate roads."

The deputy traced the roads on the map with his finger, a slow smile crossing his face. "You are indeed right."

Henderson tried to catch her eye, but Elle still

wouldn't look directly at him. He wanted to hug her for her tenacity in finding out that bit of information. "So I guess this means no one was trespassing."

"That's correct." Stubbs stared down at the map. "Since it's a county road, I suppose anyone has a right to travel the entire length, right through the heart of the farm."

That hadn't been what Henderson had expected the deputy to say, but before he could follow up on that intriguing statement, the doorbell pealed.

"Duty calls," Alec said before leaving the dining room.

Isabella stood and began clearing the dishes with Elle's assistance. Henderson decided he would ask Stubbs what he'd meant when Alec returned, followed by two women.

"Henderson," Alec said, the tone of his voice telling Henderson to brace himself, "your sister is here to see you."

EIGHTEEN

Elle froze in the back hallway at Alec's words. She hurried into the dining room, her eyes going to the two women who stood in the middle of the room. The older one she recognized as Nalani Judd, mother of Holden, whom they'd met at the hospital. Side by side, the two women shared a remarkable resemblance with the same shade of brown hair cut in similar styles and brown eyes. Helena leaned heavily on Nalani, who had her arm threaded around the younger woman's waist, as if her legs wouldn't support her otherwise.

"Helena?" Henderson rose to his feet, his attention fixed on his sister. "Is that really you?"

"Henderson." Helena's voice had a breathy quality to it, as if speaking took more energy than she possessed.

Elle peered closer at Helena, this time noting the pale skin and dull hair.

Henderson moved closer, holding out his arms to his sister. With a quick glance at Nalani, who gave the tiniest of nods, Helena launched herself into her brother's embrace.

Elle blinked back tears at the expression of hope and love on Henderson's face as he held Helena tight. She turned her attention from the happy pair to see Nalani purse her lips before smoothing out her expression when she caught Elle's gaze.

"Helena is living with you on the farm?" Elle asked Nalani.

"I had no idea her family thought she was missing," Nalani said. "When I told Helena about meeting the nice couple who had found Holden, she didn't mention she knew Henderson at all. Then someone found one of the missing persons flyers, and…well, we knew we couldn't let Helena's family think she was missing when she's been with us."

Henderson pulled back, his hand brushing moisture from Helena's cheeks. "Hey, don't cry. I missed you too."

Helena's eyes welled with tears again. "How's Mom?"

Henderson sobered. "She's not well." He explained her surgery and prognosis. "She wants to see you."

Helena shook her head. "That's not possible."

"Helena, all she wants is to hug her daughter again before she dies. That's not too much to ask. It would take a few days—"

"I said I couldn't do it." The hardness of Helena's voice made Elle jump.

Nalani touched Helena's back. "Why don't you wait in the car?"

Without another word, Helena wrenched herself from Henderson's arms and ran from the room.

"Helena!" Henderson started after her but Nalani caught his arm.

"Don't go after her," Nalani said.

Henderson shook off her hand, his eyes flicking toward the arch where his sister had fled. "You can't tell me what to do."

"No, I can't, but your sister hasn't been well," Nalani said, her voice calm and soothing.

That stopped Henderson cold. "What do you mean? Is she ill?"

"Not in the way you're thinking, but she has been battling drug addiction. We've finally gotten her to a good place where she's been clean for several years. But you saw her—she's not strong enough mentally to return to the place where she started taking drugs, even for a short visit."

Henderson crossed his arms. "My sister is a recovering drug addict, and you've been helping her get and stay clean—is that what you're saying?"

"Yes, we run a small clinic for recovering drug addicts on the farm, nothing official, just for a few people who have found their way to us over the years. The fresh air and hard work help them to heal and recover. Helena's been doing remarkably well, but hearing you're in town has brought back all of those memories and stirred up the desire for drugs again." Nalani bowed her head. "I caught her with a dose of meth two days ago. Thankfully, she hadn't taken the drug yet, but she was close."

Henderson's shoulders drooped. "I had no idea. But why hasn't she contacted her family? Why leave us in the dark, wondering if she's alive or dead?"

Nalani shook her head. "In the beginning, we encouraged her not to contact you, as that can lead to setbacks. But later, we didn't restrict who she called or didn't call. Frankly, we were as baffled as you were to learn she'd cut off all contact."

"I see," Henderson said, but Elle could tell he didn't by the set of his jaw.

"I know this is hard. It always is when your loved one is battling something as deadly as drug addiction. But I hope you will trust Helena knows what she needs," Nalani said.

"And right now, that's no contact with her family?" Frustration tinged Henderson's question.

"I'm sure she'll be in a better place soon and be able to resume calls with you and your mother. Now, if you'll excuse me, I need to get Helena back." Without waiting for a response, Nalani walked briskly out of the room.

Henderson didn't move until the front door clicked shut behind Nalani. "Drug addiction recovery, my foot."

Elle wasn't surprised at his anger. "You didn't believe her?"

"Anyone could see my sister was higher than a kite." Henderson spat the words out as he paced.

"Unfortunately, we can't arrest someone for being under the influence unless they are breaking the law," Stubbs replied, his voice mild but his eyes sharp on Henderson.

Elle concurred with Henderson's assessment of his sister's condition. Her shakiness and dilated eyes were the hallmarks of drug use. "Then why bring Helena here to see you?"

"Because there's something on the compound they don't want us to find out," Henderson said. "If they can convince me my sister is okay but doesn't want contact with me or our mom, then I would presumably head back to New York."

"But you're not going to do that." Elle wouldn't either, in his situation. Good thing she'd managed to hit the record button on her phone when she'd walked into the dining room. Something Nalani had said had tickled her brain but she couldn't put her finger on it now. Listening to the conversation again might trigger the thought.

"How can I?" Henderson whirled to face Elle, and she allowed herself to meet his anguished gaze. "Not when she's being held hostage."

Surely, Elle had misheard Henderson.

"Hostage? Are you sure?" Stubbs asked the very question Elle had thought.

Henderson's lips firmed into a grim line. "I'm sure."

"How?" Elle pressed, concerned that he was grasping at an explanation for his sister's decision to cut herself off from her family. There was something about Nalani she didn't trust, but that didn't mean she thought the woman culpable in kidnapping Helena.

"Because Helena told me." Henderson swung his gaze back to Elle, the truth blazing in his eyes. "She whispered it when she hugged me."

"She said she was being held hostage?" Stubbs's voice held disbelief.

"Not in those words." Henderson scrubbed his hand over his beard. "She told me she needed me to play Sir George."

"Sir George?" Elle scrambled to recall the significance of the name.

"Wasn't he the knight who rescued a princess from a dragon?" Isabella said. "I think one of my nephews has a children's book about it."

"Exactly," Henderson said. "We used to play that when we were kids. I was always Sir George and Helena the princess."

"So you're interpreting her words to mean she needs rescuing?" Stubbs put in.

"My sister is in trouble. For whatever reason,

she can't leave the compound on her own. You saw how Nalani managed the encounter. Telling Helena when to leave then informing us of my sister's fragile mental state," Henderson said. "Before you ask, yes, Helena used drugs, possibly to the extent of becoming an addict."

Elle tuned out while they discussed the encounter, her thoughts on why Helena couldn't leave. Her entire demeanor had been that of a frightened woman trying to put on a brave front to convince her audience she was okay. In her experience interviewing people for her podcast, the number-one reason for such behavior boiled down to protecting someone else. In the case of a woman, that someone else nine times out of ten was her child. Hazel's big, brown eyes, magnified behind her glasses, flashed side-by-side with Helena's dark ones. Hazel, who had tucked the map into her peaches. Hazel, who had braved the dogs and men patrolling the compound to make sure Elle got the map and list of names.

Could Hazel be Helena's daughter and the reason Helena had cooperated with Nalani? If that was the case, what was Nalani's role? Too many questions and not enough answers.

"Don't you think, Elle?" Henderson's query jolted Elle back to the conversation.

Her cheeks warmed as she confessed, "Sorry, I wasn't paying attention."

Henderson raised an eyebrow but didn't inquire as to what she had been thinking. "Alec and I think we should take a trip to the compound this afternoon, driving through on the county road."

Elle glanced from Alec to Henderson to Stubbs. "What does Deputy Stubbs think?"

"I'm staying out of this," Stubbs said. "Such a trip doesn't warrant the involvement of the sheriff's department in a fishing expedition. All I can say is stay on the county road and leave at the first sight of force. I don't want to be called out to investigate a death."

"Good advice," Alec said. "What if we find our way impeded by a gate or fence?"

"Then call me, as that's a clear violation of the county code, which states public roads must be open to the public at all times. I'd best be going." The deputy replaced his hat. "Thank you again for lunch, Mrs. Stratman."

The others echoed their goodbyes then Alec walked the deputy to the door.

Elle turned to Isabella. "Are you coming too?"

Isabella shook her head. "I'll stay here just in case the cavalry needs to be called in."

"Then what time do we leave?" Elle asked.

In the front seat of Alec's SUV, Henderson drew in air, held it for the count of ten, then slowly exhaled in the same time frame. He repeated the exercise twice more before his heartrate settled nearer to normal. The closer they got to County Road 4205, the tighter the band around his chest grew. The deep breaths helped but didn't alleviate his anxiety. *Lord, please let us get Helena out. Keep her and us safe. Heal my mom, so she can see Helena face-to-face. Amen.*

He hadn't called his mom after Helena's visit, not wanting to raise her hopes only to dash them when Kathleen realized Helena wouldn't be coming to New York. Better to wait until he had figured out what kept Helena unable to leave on her own. Something held his sister back. Fear for her life? Something illegal from her past that had her scared of prosecution? Somehow, neither of those scenarios fit what he remembered about his sister.

"Here we go." Alec turned left onto County Road 4205.

"There's the tree, on the left." Elle pointed from the back seat as they passed a massive V-trunked tree. "And here is where I saw the men stop the Jeep and talk to Hazel."

Alec glanced at the odometer. "About six-tenths of a mile from the main road."

Henderson peered through the windshield at the dirt-and-gravel road. "I don't see anything up ahead yet."

"The surveyor's office said 4205 is about three miles long," Elle said. "Straight through the property."

The road curved slightly to the left then back to the right in a short S shape. As Alec guided the SUV straight again, Henderson spied a gate across the road up ahead. "Looks like someone has blocked access."

Alec slowed as they approached the gate. "Those are state-of-the-art cameras monitoring whoever approaches."

From the back seat, Elle said, "I'm calling the deputy to report the gate."

Alec brought the vehicle to a stop.

"Should we get out or stay in the car?" Henderson didn't see anyone in the vicinity.

Alec drummed his fingers on the steering wheel. "Stay put. I don't like that we're essentially sitting ducks here."

"I had to leave a message," Elle said.

"I think we have company now," Alec said.

Dust billowed as a vehicle sped toward the gate, the driver braking hard. The same two men who had responded to their approach at the other gate stepped out and walked toward the gate.

Henderson reached for the door handle. "Let me talk to them." He turned to Alec. "You can cover me with your rifle if necessary."

"I don't like it. I think we should leave and come back with Stubbs," Alec said.

"I agree with Alec," Elle said. "Something feels off."

Henderson opened the door. "I'll be careful." He climbed out before either one could utter another word of protest. "Good afternoon," he called to the two men, ignoring the rifles each held pointed in his general direction.

"I thought we told you this is private property," the driver snapped, his eyes hidden behind aviator shades.

"Actually, it isn't." Henderson kept his tone pleasant, as if he were discussing the weather. "This is County Road 4205, which is a public thoroughfare. As such, county code prohibits blocking the public from using the road at any time."

Neither man responded to his statement. Then the driver hung the rifle over his shoulder by its strap and dialed a number on his phone. Henderson waited, taking in as many details as possible while the driver completed his call in a voice too low for Henderson to hear. When the driver replaced the phone in his pocket but made no move to unlock the gate, Henderson prompted, "Please open the gate so we can be on our way."

Both men didn't move or speak. Henderson walked over to the gate's locking system, pulling out his phone. A keypad instead of a keyed lock secured the gate. Several more cameras filmed the approach on the opposite side. Interesting. To keep tabs on who was coming and going? He snapped photos of the security measures.

"Hey, you can't do that!" The second man charged up to the gate, anger sparking in his dark eyes.

Henderson didn't let the man's agitation ruffle him. "I'm on public land and there's no laws against taking photos."

"That's proprietary technology," the man said. "You can't take photos of that."

Henderson typed the security firm's name into Safari, then turned his phone to display the results, which showed a variety of similar locks. "As you can see, the company itself has photos of its lock systems online, so I hardly think my snapping photos would constitute stealing the technology."

"Dameon, that's enough," the driver called.

Dameon narrowed his eyes and kept his mouth shut. A black SUV drove up, parking beside the Jeep. A man with a shaved head exited the front passenger seat and then opened the back door.

The boss himself, if Henderson had to guess. The man who exited wore dark blue dress pants and a crisp, button-down bright blue shirt with an open collar. Henderson noted the expensive leather boots. The driver hurried over to greet the newcomer while the shaved-head man stood sentry. Personal security. Interesting.

The driver and newcomer came toward Henderson.

"I think there's been a misunderstanding," the newcomer said, his voice a pleasant baritone.

"No misunderstanding," Henderson replied, matching the tenor of the other man's voice. "My companions and I wish to drive on this public road. Your gate is stopping us."

The newcomer smiled. "My apologies, I should have introduced myself. I'm Obadiah Judd. I believe you met my wife, Nalani, earlier today when she brought your sister to see you."

Henderson had expected his identity to be figured out rather quickly, so the man's statement didn't alarm him. "Ah, Mr. Judd. Yes, I met Mrs. Judd." He didn't mention his sister, not sure he could trust himself not to demand to see her.

"Are you sure this little jaunt isn't more about wanting to see Helena again than merely taking a drive?" Judd said.

Henderson let the question hang in the air while he considered his reply. "My motive doesn't matter. The law says all county roads are to be accessible to the public at all times, and this is a county road."

"Ah, but the county road in question has to be in use for the law to apply," Judd countered. "No one uses this road anymore, not since the state put in the bypass a dozen or so years ago."

Henderson wanted to wipe the smirk off Judd's face, but didn't want to give the other man the satisfaction of seeing him lose his cool. "Use doesn't matter. The deed to this property clearly marks this as a county road."

Another vehicle approached from behind Henderson, halting the conversation. Deputy Stubbs exited a sheriff's car and headed for the gate. "I'm Deputy Stubbs," he said, extending his hand to Judd. "I don't believe we've met."

Judd introduced himself to Stubbs.

"Mr. Parker, what seems to be the problem?" Stubbs asked.

Henderson explained the predicament.

"Mr. Judd, open the gate please and let these people drive through." Stubbs might have smiled when he gave the command, but Henderson caught the steel behind it.

For a second, Henderson thought Judd would refuse, then the man shrugged and moved to the gate. Punching in a code at the keypad, the gate swung open. "Be my guest. But please remember to stay on the road. Anything else is trespassing."

Henderson nodded. "Thank you." He climbed back into the SUV. "Drive on." He tucked away his frustration at not catching a glimpse of Helena. Instead, he focused on figuring out his next steps. One way or another, he was getting his sister out of this place.

NINETEEN

The grandfather clock in the front hallway struck one as Henderson crept down the stairs, boots in one hand and a backpack in the other. Moonlight spilled through the narrow windows on either side of the front door, casting eerie shadows on the foyer. After the drive through the compound had revealed no sign of buildings or people, he had decided a stealth approach would be best. Not wanting to involve Alec or Isabella in trespassing on compound property, he'd spent the afternoon and evening gathering supplies and planning. He sat on the bottom step and put on his hiking boots as he mentally reviewed his supplies tucked into a small pack. Flashlight. Phone turned on dark mode. Wire cutters. Travel first-aid kit.

"Going somewhere?"

Henderson jumped at the sound of Elle's voice floating down from above him. He twisted to see her descending the stairs, fully dressed in the same outfit she'd worn Saturday night, a dark backpack on one shoulder.

"I am." No sense trying to obscure the truth. She could easily see he wasn't dressed for a midnight snack.

"I'm going with you." She joined him on the step, sitting close enough that he could brush the strand of hair off her cheek without stretching.

But he didn't. Instead, he tried to dissuade her from accompanying him. "It's too dangerous."

"Sir George might have slayed the dragon alone, but you shouldn't attempt to rescue your sister by yourself."

He wouldn't acknowledge he had qualms himself about venturing to the compound solo. Bending to finish tying his laces, he said, "It will be hard enough to slip in and out undetected. With two of us, it might prove impossible."

"Yes, but you aren't rescuing just Helena."

Her matter-of-fact statement made him jerk his gaze to meet hers. "What do you mean?"

"Why do you think Helena hasn't come home?"

"Because they keep her high on drugs." The certainty of that statement boiled his blood. He would get his sister out then make sure Judd and his gang paid for what they'd done to Helena.

Elle shook her head. "That's only a very small part. Helena's strong, like you. She would be able to kick the habit if she had a safe place to do so."

That was what had angered him about his sister all those years ago—her resolve not to get help. Deep down, he knew her capable of overcoming her addiction, but only if she wanted to. "Then what's keeping her there?"

"Her daughter."

The words rocked him to his feet. "What?"

Elle stood. "It's the only explanation that makes any sense."

Henderson rubbed a hand over his beard. "It doesn't to me."

"What's the one thing a mother will rarely do of her own free will?"

A flash of insight sparked in his brain. "Leave her child in an unsafe environment."

"Exactly. Helena's protecting someone. Hazel slipped me the map to the tree, and I saw her check the papers inside the tree. Who put Hazel up to that?"

"Her mother." With that information, Helena's actions during her visit and her phone call begging them to stay away made perfect sense. His sister was trying to protect her daughter. "We need to get Hazel and Helena out."

"And that's why you need me." Elle extracted something from her pocket, moving to the small circular table in the middle of the foyer. "I photocopied the map Helena had drawn at the copy store this afternoon onto one piece of paper."

Spreading the large sheet flat, she pointed to

the house. "This is where I think Hazel is." Tapping the bushes near the house, she added, "See the faces here?"

He peered closely and discerned the frightened countenances of several children cleverly disguised in the foliage. "Okay. What about Helena?"

"My best guess is here." She indicated the barn. "There's a *X* on the side."

"That's how she always marked our treasure maps, with a curly *X*." His eyes misted at the *X* nearly hidden in the lines of the barn's front doors.

"Now what's the plan?"

Henderson fingered the bag of raw meat in his pocket, hoping the double layers of plastic kept it from leaking. If they encountered those dogs, he wanted to be prepared. Beside him, Elle placed her feet carefully, her eyes on the ground to avoid snapping a twig and giving away their position. They'd parked near the Gray farm, and approached the property from the woods. Walking the perimeter of the fence line, he searched for an easy way over or through the chain link.

The good news was that they'd spotted no cameras, except for those guarding the gates.

She touched his arm and he halted. "I think the house should be straight ahead," she whispered. Through the trees on the other side of the fence, he glimpsed a clearing. "I think you're right." He slowly lowered his backpack, extracting a pair of wire cutters. "Ready?"

During the drive over, they had decided Elle would get Hazel, while he would go after Helena, then meet at a designated spot. She nodded, moving away to give him room to work. In short order, he had an opening cut. Replacing the tool in the backpack, he shouldered it. "You go first." He peeled back the fencing enough for Elle to slip through and then followed her.

On the other side, both stood still, listening, but only the occasional hoot of an owl greeted their arrival. His heart pounded. In all his years, he'd never flagrantly broken the law. Now he could be arrested for trespassing—but only if he got caught. For Helena's sake, he couldn't let that happen.

Together, they moved as quietly as possible through the trees, stopping at the tree line about fifty feet from the fence. Just as Elle had predicted, the house and barn, along with a shed, occupied the clearing. All buildings were dark. Henderson scanned the house then nudged Elle to point out the security lights on the porch and side of the building. She nodded and motioned she would go.

Before she could take a step, he grabbed her hand, pulling her close. He couldn't let her go without telling her how he felt. Since talking would be foolish so close to the buildings, he placed his lips over hers. She stiffened then her body relaxed into his and she kissed him back. Reluctantly, he broke the contact, smoothing back some hair from her face before stealing a second kiss. Then he whirled her around and gave her a little push in the direction of the house.

For a moment, she didn't advance, then she squared her shoulders and stepped out of the trees. He wanted to watch her but knew for their plan to work, he had to get to the barn as quickly as possible. Lord willing, there would be time to discuss that kiss—and their future—when they had Hazel and Helena safe.

As silently as possible, he darted across the grass and to the side of the barn without setting off a motion detector. Hugging the wall, he inched toward the back of the barn, managing to stay in the security light's blind spot. As he had suspected, the barn had a small back door set on the side closest to Henderson. A keypad lock secured it. Slipping on a pair of surgical gloves, he took a deep breath and tried the combination he'd seen Judd use to open the gate. Judd hadn't realized Henderson had recorded his actions. Watching the video later had given him several ideas as to the sequence of numbers, guessing that no one liked to have too many different combinations to remember.

The lock clicked and Henderson pulled open

the door, slipping inside and closing it quietly. He didn't move immediately, standing with his back to the door to get his bearings and allow his eyes to adjust to the barn's interior. Security lamps gave off a low glow, providing enough light to decipher furnishings. As he and Elle had suspected, the barn had been converted into living quarters.

He was standing in a large industrial kitchen, a gleaming six-burner stove, double oven, and metal work tables dominating the open area. A walk-in fridge stood beside a similar freezer. Shelving held dry goods and kitchenware. Leaning to one side, he could make out a long farm table with benches on either side occupying one side of the room while a sectional couch and love seats grouped around a massive flat-screen TV was on the other. Several closed doors led to what he thought must be bathrooms and sleeping quarters. But how to tell which one Helena was in without waking up all of the occupants?

He'd not advanced beyond the kitchen when an alarm split the air.

The house proved impenetrable without triggering a security light. Elle had managed to make it to the corner of the structure without detection, but the porch had several lights aimed in all directions, and the back entrance boasted the same level of security. Cameras accompanied the lights, and she couldn't be sure she hadn't been caught on camera in her approach. Her options were to abandon her mission, boldly walk up to the house and demand to see Hazel, or come up with a plan C. If only she could get Hazel to come to her…

Elle squatted and reached under the bushes that hugged the side of the house. Despite the rainstorm a few nights ago, the brush was pretty dry. Tilting her head back, she examined the windows on this side of the house. The first floor ones were closed, but a few on the upper story were open.

An idea formed. It was bold and audacious, but it might just work. No time to text Henderson her plan. Pulling a small box of matches from a survival kit she'd tossed in her backpack, she struck one then tossed the lit match into the brush. Repeating the exercise along the line of bushes, she soon had a good blaze going. Smoke rose to the sky while flames gobbled up the bushes.

Elle moved toward the front door, not worrying about the security lights or cameras as the smoke swirled around the house. Within minutes, an alarm pierced the air, shrill and insistent. She heard an echo of the alarm and realized the system must be tied into the barn. Lights flicked on in both the barn and house. She crouched beside the front porch as far from the flames as she could manage without being immediately visible to anyone exiting the house or barn.

"The bushes are on fire," a female voice said above Elle on the porch. "We'd better evacuate the house."

People streamed out of the barn, some huddling together near a tall oak tree while others raced toward the back of the house. Elle kept her eyes on those coming down the porch steps. Soon, she spotted two women shepherding a group of children to the oak tree, which must be the evacuation gathering place.

Then someone shouted for help with a bucket brigade. In the ensuing chaos of people rushing toward and around the house, Elle slipped from her hiding place and joined the exodus to the tree. She stayed on the fringes as the two women tried to settle the children, many of which started crying.

Hazel stood near the edge of the cluster, clasping hands with a boy. Elle recognized Holden, the child she and Henderson had found by the side of the road. The Judd boy must be of an age with Hazel. Coming up behind the pair, she gently touched Hazel's shoulder. The girl turned, her eyes widening behind her glasses. Elle put her finger to her lips for silence, and the girl didn't utter a sound. She poked Holden, who gaped at Elle.

Elle dropped to a crouch. "Hazel, we're here to take you and your mother away from here."

The little girl violently shook her head and

threw her arms around Holden, who hugged her hard. The two, Hazel in a cartoon princess nightdress and Holden in superhero summer PJs, glared defiantly at Elle. In that moment, she realized she'd made a terrible mistake. "You're twins."

Hazel snuffled, wiping the back of her hand across her nose. "He's my brother."

"And Helena is your mother?" Elle wanted to be sure.

Both kids nodded.

"Then let's go." She stood, a hand on either child's shoulder.

"You won't be going anywhere."

TWENTY

Henderson barely had time to slip behind some open shelving in the kitchen when the inner doors burst open. Men and women, some fully dressed and others in pajamas, spilled into the common area. Many of the men sported the snake tattoo, as did quite a few of the women.

One of the men pointed to the house. "There's a fire at the house. We need to get dressed and go help put it out." His words galvanized the group, and many returned to their rooms, presumably to dress, while others headed for the rear door—and Henderson's hiding place. The back door opened. Through the shelves, Henderson made out the newcomer as Dameon.

Henderson sucked in his breath and squeezed as far back as he could between two metal shelves full of dry goods. If anyone turned their head while walking by toward the back door, they might spot him.

"Everyone who's able, please go to the house

to help with the bucket brigade. Everyone else, meet at the evacuation point," Dameon said.

People started asking him questions about the fire as they followed him out. With a break in the flow, Henderson made his way outside and around the far side of the barn to regroup. Rounding the building, he paused to scan the yard for the evacuation meeting point. The growing crowd of people under a large tree indicated the spot. Elle appeared on the edge of the group, talking to two children. She must have found Hazel.

His heart plummeted to his stomach when a figure separated from the crowd and circled the tree to come up behind Elle.

"Ready to join your friend?"

The muzzle of a gun in the small of his back made him stiffen. He recognized the driver's voice, along with the hard edge that said he would be delighted if Henderson resisted. The man directed him toward the shed at the back of the clearing. Henderson wanted to keep a close eye on Elle, but he lost sight of her and the children in the milieu. The driver shoved Henderson through the shed door, letting it close with a bang behind them.

The shed was much larger than Henderson had thought from the outside. An open area with several tables and chairs, a small fridge, and a TV mounted on one wall took up most of the space, with a hallway leading back to other rooms.

The driver frisked Henderson, removing the bag of meat from his pocket with a smirk, then shoved him into a chair. "Don't move."

The door opened and Nalani Judd dragged Elle inside, followed by another woman hauling a girl and Holden. Both kids sniffled, tears running down their cheeks. Nalani pushed Elle into a chair at another table.

"You said we didn't have to worry about these two," Nalani snarled.

The driver shrugged. "Stubbs told me he was keeping a close eye on them."

Henderson couldn't keep the surprise from his face.

The driver saw it and smiled, a mean gesture that made his eyes glitter with malice. "That's right. Deputy Stubbs has been working against you."

Through the door, Obadiah Judd brought Helena, his hand gripping her upper arm. He tossed her to the floor, where she landed in a heap. The children broke out of their minder's loose hold and fell to their knees beside Helena.

"Mama!" Holden cried, his arms reaching for Helena as she sat up.

"Are you okay, Mama?" the little girl said, her voice tremulous.

Henderson reeled from their words. Two children? He looked more closely at the size of the kids. Twins.

Judd yanked Holden up. "You are not to call her that!" He shook the boy once, hard enough that Holden's head snapped back. "She is your mother." Judd pointed to his wife, who surveyed the group with a serene expression.

Holden's lip quivered but the defiant look in his eyes reminded Henderson so much of Helena, that he almost pitied Judd. "She is not!"

"That's enough, my dear." Nalani strolled over to her husband. "Leave it for now. We have other things to attend to."

Judd gave Holden one more shake before depositing the boy back on the ground near Helena, who gathered him and the girl—who must be Hazel—in her arms.

Dameon came into the shed. "The fire has been extinguished."

"Good," Judd said. "Mitch, please inform the fire department we don't need their services."

The driver nodded, pulling out his phone and making a call while Dameon took up a post by the door, crossing his beefy arms.

Henderson tried to catch Elle's eye, but she was looking at Helena and the two kids.

Helena struggled to her feet, grasping the back of a chair for balance. "Let them go."

"It's a little too late for that, isn't it?" Judd growled, pointing a finger at Helena. "You will be punished for not convincing your brother to leave you alone."

Helena bent at the waist, her sobs tearing at Henderson's heart. "No, no, no. Please…"

Henderson surged to his feet, wanting to comfort his sister, but Mitch cocked a handgun at him and Henderson sank back into the chair.

"What are you going to do with us?" Elle asked. "Dope us up like you've been doing to Helena? Will we have an unfortunate overdose like Rose McCellan?"

"How do you know about Rose?" Judd barked, striding toward Elle.

"We were at the clinic with Holden when her husband burst in demanding to see Rose." Elle leaned forward. "But she was already dead of an overdose. Her poor husband insisted she never took too much."

"Druggies are always lying about something," Judd spat out. "Who can you believe?"

A knock on the door drew Henderson's attention. Dameon opened it and admitted Deputy Stubbs, whose gaze swept the room before coming back to rest on Henderson.

"Thought you'd be trouble," Stubbs said.

"Caught the pair of them trespassing," Mitch said. "And we have her on video, starting the fire."

Henderson swiveled to Elle, impressed with her ingenuity.

"You can add arson to the charges against her," Judd said.

"Noted," Stubbs replied. "Let's go, you two."

"I came for my sister, and I'm not leaving without her." Henderson paused. "Or my niece and nephew."

Helena's sobs had quieted. At her brother's words, she straightened. "I'm coming with you."

"That's your choice," Judd said, "but Hazel and Holden will not accompany you."

"They're my children!" The desperation in Helena's voice chilled Henderson to the core.

"You're not fit to be their mother. Look at you. Strung out all the time," Judd mocked. "No, the children are better off here."

"You have no claim on them." But at the look in his sister's eyes, Henderson knew why Judd had such confidence in his assertion the twins would stay at the compound.

"Ah, she didn't tell you, did she?" Judd rubbed his hands together, clearly relishing the moment of his big reveal. "I'm their father."

Elle had been expecting Judd to say that, given his wife's statement about Holden being her son.

Helena hung her head, shame dripping from her posture like Spanish moss hanging from a tree.

"I'm sorry," Helena whispered. "He's right. He's their father."

Henderson clamped his mouth shut, as if bottling words he would regret saying. Elle turned to look at Nalani. The woman stood off to the side, a very pleased smile gracing her lips. Strange, the wife would take such pleasure in hearing about her husband's infidelity. Most would not want it thrown in their faces, yet Nalani didn't appear perturbed at all.

Elle wanted to shake the woman's composure and see what happened. "What do you think of your husband's infidelity, Nalani?"

Nalani's smile widened. "I trust my husband implicitly. He would never do anything to deliberately harm me."

A very strange statement, but before Elle could push her more, Stubbs interrupted. "Will you be pressing charges against Mr. Parker and Ms. Updike for trespassing and attempted arson?"

"To the full extent of the law," Judd replied, his eyes gleaming with satisfaction.

Stubbs reached for his handcuffs when his phone rang. He pulled it out. "It's the sheriff. I'd better take this outside." He stepped out of the room.

"What about the meth labs?" Elle blurted, not willing to leave Helena to her fate without one last try.

"What are you talking about?" Judd demanded. "There are no meth labs here."

"Really?" Elle cocked her head as if considering. "You don't know, do you? Amazing." She turned to Mitch, who glared back. "You know about the meth labs, and I'm betting Dameon knows too."

Elle let her gaze travel back to Judd. "But if you don't know, then you're not the boss."

"Of course I'm in charge! Who do you think you're talking to?" Judd shook his finger in her face, his own scarlet with anger.

Elle brushed off his taunts, instead focusing on Nalani. "It's you. You're the one running the meth labs. I'll bet you're the brains of this entire operation."

Nalani arranged her mouth into a smug expression Elle wanted to wipe off her face. But if the meth lab accusation didn't shake the woman, and her husband's confession of infidelity didn't, then what would? All of a sudden, she knew. "Too bad your success didn't extend to having your own child."

Nalani narrowed her eyes.

Elle laughed. "That's why you keep Helena drugged up—so you can play mommy with her children. What's the matter? Can't have any of your own so you had to steal someone else's?"

"I'm raising my husband's out-of-wedlock children as my own," Nalani snapped. "Most people would say that makes me a good person."

"You'd like to think so." From the thinning of Nalani's lips, Elle could see her words were beginning to rattle the woman. Time to press home her meager advantage. "Obadiah isn't really the father, is he?"

"Of course he is." Nalani's eyes flashed fire.

Elle continued as if she hadn't spoken, putting a plausible theory out into the open. "Did you discover Helena was pregnant and decided to trick your husband into thinking he'd slept with her so you could claim her baby as your own?"

"Is that true?" Judd stared at his wife. "I always said I didn't remember touching Helena, but you insisted that I had."

"She's lying, trying to break our family apart," Nalani said, her higher pitch indicating how rattled she was. "If I'd left it up to you, I would still not be a mother."

Judd sank into a chair opposite Henderson, dropping his head into his hands. "What have you done?"

"What you didn't have the guts to do," his wife said.

Watching the dynamic between husband and wife, Elle decided to push the wedge in deeper between them. "Did you know your wife was testing a new batch of meth, one more potent than before?"

Judd raised his head. "What?"

Nalani whirled on Elle, some of her earlier confidence returning. "Uh-uh-uh," she chided, shaking her finger back and forth. "You don't know anything."

"I know how many people have died after sampling your drugs." Elle rattled off the names with asterisks beside them that she recalled from the sheet of paper. "How else are you paying for all of this? It's certainly not from selling produce and a few toys at a farmers market."

"You can't prove any of it, and I'm getting tired of your chatter," Nalani said. "Mitch?"

The driver approached Elle, poking the gun at her. "Get up." Then Mitch nodded to Dameon. "Get Parker."

Dameon advanced on Henderson and punched him in the head.

Elle gasped as Henderson fell out of his chair and onto the floor. "Henderson!"

Mitch shoved his gun into her side. "Don't move."

Dameon kicked Henderson in the ribs. "Get up."

Henderson groaned and rolled over, bracing himself against a table to stand.

"Wait a minute." Judd stood. "In the south field, the shed you built to store produce over the winter. The one with the state-of-the-art ventilation system. That's not for apples."

Nalani huffed. "Don't get all righteous on me, Obadiah."

"So it's true." The hurt look on Judd's face might have touched Elle's heart if the man's ignorance hadn't cost people their lives.

Once Henderson gained his feet, Dameon prodded him with his rifle toward the door. "Let's go."

"No." Judd spoke the word with the authority of a man used to being obeyed.

Mitch turned to Nalani. "Mrs. Judd?"

Judd's mouth dropped open at the clear show of loyalty for his wife over him. "Mitch?"

"Sorry, Mr. Judd, but Mrs. Judd outranks you." Mitch dug the gun into Elle's ribs.

Elle bit back a cry of pain as Mitch propelled her toward the door. "She'll take care of you next, Obadiah. She's not going to leave any loose ends!"

"I want answers, and I want them now, Nalani." Judd faced his wife.

Elle struggled to free herself from Mitch's grip, but the man didn't yield. Twisting her body, Elle saw Dameon shove Henderson in the same direction.

"You want answers?" Nalani scoffed. "While you spouted nonsense with your Copperheads, I've been planning a real revolution."

"A drug revolution?" Elle called over her shoulder as Mitch dragged her closer to the door.

"Yes. People dependent on drugs will do anything to get their next fix. I was perfecting the formula that would make them want my meth forever." Nalani smiled, but her hard gaze landed on Henderson. "Something Helena should know about, eh?"

"You didn't give her a choice!" Henderson said. "I won't let you keep her a prisoner." He elbowed Dameon in the stomach, momentarily stunning the other man.

Mitch took a step toward Dameon, his grip loosening a fraction on her arm. Elle took advantage of Mitch's distraction to turn into his body and bring up her knee with all her strength. Her aim proved true. Mitch doubled over, dropping his hand from her arm. Taking a step back, she kicked out and sent Mitch's gun flying from his hand.

Henderson and Dameon grappled for Dameon's rifle.

With a cry, Helena launched herself at Nalani, catching the older woman off guard. The two women fell to the floor, Helena clawing and scratching while Nalani attempted to cover her face with her hands.

Elle squatted beside Holden and Hazel. "Let's get you out of here." She rose, holding the hand of each child.

Then door flew open with a bang and men in tactical SWAT gear swarmed into the space. Multiple voices shouted, "Freeze! FBI!"

Elle dropped to her knees, circling her arms around the children to shield them as men and women poured into the room. The twins clung to her, their bodies shaking as she murmured over and over again, "It's over. It's finally over."

TWENTY-ONE

Henderson held the ice pack to his throbbing cheek while the EMT dabbed disinfectant on the back of his hand where the rifle had scraped it during his tussle with Dameon. At a nearby table, Elle sat talking quietly with Hazel and Holden, juice boxes in front of the kids, while another EMT checked Helena across the room. A long red scratch trailed down the length of her pale face. His sister kept turning her head to check on the twins, as if she couldn't bear to let them out of her sight.

"Keep the ice on for another ten minutes," the EMT advised him. "See a doctor tomorrow if anything changes."

"Thanks." Henderson rose and moved to Elle's table. "How are you holding up?"

"As well as can be expected," she said. "I don't think you've been formally introduced. Holden, Hazel, this is your uncle Henderson."

The kids smiled, Hazel ducking her head.

Holden met his gaze. "You helped me by the side of the road."

"Yes, I did," Henderson replied. "I wasn't sure you remembered."

The boy nodded. "Mama told me where to find you. I forgot to take water with me, and then I had to hide in the woods ever so long until the coast was clear. That's why I was so tired and thirsty."

Henderson ruffled the boy's hair. "It's okay. We're glad we found you in time."

Holden's eyes filled with tears. "We won't have to stay here, will we?"

"No." Henderson reassured his nephew. "Your mom's probably going to need to stay somewhere else for a while, but you and your sister will come home with me and meet your grandmother. She's very anxious to say hello."

Hazel's eyes brightened. "Is the treehouse still there? Mama told us about all the adventures you and she had there."

"I'll have to make sure it's seaworthy, but yes, it's still up in the old oak tree." Henderson hadn't thought of the treehouse his father had built for him and his sister for their ninth birthdays in years. "Did she tell you about the secret room?"

The twins shook their heads, eyes round.

Henderson entertained them with a story about the secret hiding place their father had built into the treehouse without telling Helena or him. By the time he'd finished, Helena had come over, supported by the EMT, who helped her into a chair.

"Mama!" Holden and Hazel both snuggled up on either side of her, their affection for Helena warming Henderson's heart. "Uncle Henderson told us all about the secret hiding place in the treehouse," Holden said, his eyes sparkling. "Do you think we'll be able to find it?"

"I'm sure you will." Helena smoothed the hair back from his forehead. "Thank you, Sir George."

Henderson blinked back sudden tears. "I couldn't leave a damsel in distress."

Helena held out her hand and Henderson grasped it tightly. "I'll need to go to a detox center, maybe for a long time. Nalani kept me hooked on the drugs for years." A tear spilled down her cheek.

"How did you meet Obadiah and Nalani?" Elle asked.

Helena sighed. "Out in the woods, near where they had some property. I used to party there." A shadow crossed her face. "Then I got pregnant, by who, I don't know. I don't remember sleeping with Obadiah, but I was so high most of the time, I can't be sure I didn't. When Nalani found out about the babies, she helped me get clean, and talked me into moving down to Virginia with her and her husband. I gave birth at home with a midwife, and I had no idea for weeks that Nalani was passing off the twins as her own."

Henderson squeezed his sister's hand as her tale unfolded. When Helena had protested Nalani's co-opting of the babies, Nalani had reintroduced her to meth and had kept her on it ever since. If Helena ever tried to contact her family, Nalani threatened to take the twins away, saying she was an unfit mother and would never see Hazel or Holden again.

"Then you came to town," Helena said. "My big brother riding to the rescue again."

"He never gave up," Elle said. "He insisted you would not have disappeared without a trace on your own."

"But if it wasn't for Elle and her podcast, I never would have found you," Henderson added. "She was instrumental in tracking down your whereabouts."

Helena swiveled her head to look from Henderson to Elle and back to her brother. "I see."

In those two words, Henderson heard something of the old Helena, the one who'd teased him about girls he liked.

"Ms. Parker, the FBI is ready to take your and your children's statements," Deputy Stubbs said, two agents in dark blue suits and crisp white shirts standing behind him. "We'll let your brother know where to find you when you've finished."

Helena nodded, rising a bit unsteadily, Hazel and Holden on either side. "Tell Mom I love her."

"I will," Henderson promised.

"I'm sure you're wondering my role in all of this," Stubbs said as he sank into Helena's empty chair.

"You were working undercover for the feds," Elle guessed.

"The lady got it in one," Stubbs said. "FBI Special Agent Barnaby Stubbs, at your service."

Henderson shook his head. "Alec said you were hiding something. He warned me to be careful around you."

Stubbs laughed. "I could tell he wasn't completely buying my deputy act."

"Were you undercover to investigate the drugs or the Copperheads?" Elle asked.

"The Copperheads. We've been concerned about the growing influence of this group, which started out as a grassroots organization but has since become more centralized. Obadiah Judd was setting himself up as the leader of the East Coast Copperheads, with grandiose ideas of building his own utopia," Stubbs said.

"They didn't seem all that organized to me," Henderson said.

"They weren't, but they could become that under the right leader," Stubbs said. "And Judd might have been that leader, if his wife's little meth empire hadn't drawn the attention of law enforcement."

"Why did she start making meth?" Elle said.

"For the money and control." Stubbs set his hat on the table. "Judd needed cash to attract more followers, and these people knew nothing of farming. Nalani had already been buying meth from a couple of the local dealers, and decided she could make a better product, generate money, and keep Helena off balance enough not to cause trouble about the twins."

"Only she hadn't quite got the formula right, and ended up causing several deaths, which got the authorities interested in what was going on," Henderson said.

"On the heels of that, you come to town threatening to break up her little family, and Nalani has a much bigger problem on her hands," Stubbs said. "Dameon's already singing, pointing the finger at Nalani for the brains behind the break-in, mugging, car chase, shooting, and attempted arson."

"Sad what someone will do to hold on to what they think should be theirs," Elle said.

"It is indeed," Stubbs agreed, checking his phone. "I've got to go brief my boss, and you two will need to talk separately to the FBI about what happened last night. Agents Willowby and Brendt will be here in a few minutes to take you to the sheriff's office, where the FBI is conducting interviews."

After Stubbs had gone, Henderson leaned back in his chair. Helena was safe. She had a long recovery ahead, but he and his mom would be there every step of the way, helping with Hazel and Holden, and holding Helena's hand. They would get through this together.

Across the table, Elle had her eyes closed. Despite her obvious fatigue, she had never looked more beautiful. Without her, he never would have found Helena. Gratitude swelled in his heart at the gift God had given him by directing Elle back into his life. He'd allowed his foolish pride to stand in the way of accepting her help two years ago, and he'd nearly let that same pride stop him from working with her this time. As Alec had pointed out, he needed to stop fighting his feelings for her and embrace them. Now that Helena was back in the family fold, the freedom to fully live his own life welled up inside him. His guilt over failing to find Helena had eaten away at his ability to have a relationship with anyone, leaving him with a hollow hole where his heart had been.

Until Elle.

The urge to tell her how he felt had him leaning toward her. For a moment, he simply drank in the sight of her tousled hair, her eyelashes sweeping against her cheeks. It was a vista a man could get used to seeing every day. He touched her hand.

She blinked, her eyes focusing on him. "Did I fall asleep?"

"Maybe for a minute." He cleared his throat. "Elle, I—"

"Mr. Parker? Ms. Updike? I'm Special Agent Willowby, and this is Special Agent Brendt." A tall man wearing a gray suit and conservative blue tie stood by their table, a woman in black slacks, white blouse and black pinstriped blazer by his side.

Henderson nearly growled in frustration, knowing he would have to put off his conversation with Elle until after they were questioned by the FBI.

"If you'll come this way, we'll go to the sheriff's office now," Agent Willowby said.

"My SUV is parked near the Gray farm," Henderson said.

"If you'll give me your keys, I'll have someone drive it to the B and B for you," Agent Brendt said.

Henderson considered protesting, but given how tired he was—and with several hours at least of questioning ahead of him—he handed over the key fob. "Thanks."

As he and Elle followed the two agents out into the morning sunlight, he prayed that Elle wouldn't slip away without his telling her what was in his heart.

Reclined on the chaise longue in the backyard of Tall Trees, Elle closed her eyes, allowing the sun to warm her face. In the three days since Helena and the twins' rescue, she'd hardly exchanged more than two words with Henderson.

After spending nearly the entire day with the FBI going over and over what had happened at the compound, she'd returned to the B and B and collapsed into bed, sleeping for more than twelve hours straight.

Then she'd spent hours on the phone with Caren, plotting the third season and scrambling for interviews. Her voice, while still raspy at times, had returned mostly to normal, allowing her to record the interviews with locals and others who'd interacted with the Judds and those living on the compound.

Henderson had texted her with his whereabouts—settling Helena into an in-patient drug treatment center near Buffalo, then bringing the twins to meet his mother. He'd said he would be back in Twin Oaks to pack the rest of Helena's things once the FBI cleared it, but Elle wasn't sure if she would still be in town then.

"Want a glass of iced tea?" Isabella set down two frosty glasses, a twig of fresh mint in both, on the table beside Elle.

"Thanks." Elle took a sip. "Ah, very refreshing."

Isabella smiled then turned to go.

"Aren't you joining me?" Elle pointed to the second glass.

"No, but I think you'll have company very soon." Isabella nodded at the house, where Henderson stood talking to Alec.

Elle's heart did a little twirl at the sight of Henderson. His beard hugged his face, outlining a strong jawline. His formfitting T-shirt and well-worn jeans accentuated his lanky frame.

As if sensing her gaze, Henderson turned and winked at her, the gesture bringing a blush to her cheeks. She held the cold glass of tea against one of her hot cheeks as he clapped Alec on the shoulder then headed her way.

Stay calm. Don't swoon. But her warnings did nothing to slow her racing pulse.

"This seat taken?" Henderson pointed to the lounge next to hers.

"Be my guest." Elle drank some tea and then set the glass on the table. "Isabella made some iced tea for you as well."

He glanced at the untouched glass. "Looks good." But he made no move to pick it up. Instead, his eyes roved over her face, an intense expression that made her want to whip out a mirror to see if she had a mint leaf stuck in her teeth.

"How is Helena settling in at the detox facility?"

Her question seemed to surprise him, as he tensed then relaxed. "Good, I think. She seems very committed to kicking the habit and getting better."

"How's your mom getting on with Hazel and Holden?" Elle slipped on her sunglasses, not wanting to give away her feelings to this man.

"While they miss their mom, they are enjoying hearing all about Helena's youthful escapades. My mom looks years younger, and the doctor said having Helena safe and grandkids in the house has been better for her recovery than any medication he could prescribe."

"I'm so glad." She pinned a smile on her face, forcing the next bit out. "I guess that means you'll be heading home for good soon."

"Tomorrow. I'm driving back with Helena's and the twins' things." He shook his head. "I still can't believe we found her. If it hadn't been for you…"

"I do love a happy ending, and my listeners do too." Elle covered up the hurt at the thought of never seeing Henderson again. "I'm sure you have a million things to do to get ready for the long drive to New York, so I'll let you get to it." She stood, picking up her half-empty glass.

Henderson jumped to his feet as well. "Please don't rush off."

She froze, her cheeks beginning to throb from the effort of keeping her smile in place. "I'll have Caren contact you and Kathleen about follow-up interviews in a week or so. Do you think Helena would be able to speak to us then?"

"Elle, I don't want to talk about my sister or the twins or the podcast. I want to talk about us."

"Us?" The word squeaked out of her. "There is no 'us.'"

He gently removed the glass from her hand, setting it back on the table beside his own. "Tell me I'm not the only one who felt a connection between us."

"I, uh…" Her voice trailed off as he placed his hands on her shoulders.

"Even before we found Helena, I wanted to tell you that I was wrong."

"You were?" Elle found it difficult to follow the conversation, the sensation of his hands rubbing up and down her upper arms filling her with a warm, fuzzy feeling.

"Yes, I never should have pushed you away." He drew her closer, shifting a hand to the small of her back. He brushed a tendril of hair behind her ear. "I'm sorry for causing you pain. Can you forgive me?"

"Yes." She sighed the word as his hand made circles on her back.

"You are an amazing woman, Elle Updike." His lips brushed against her cheek. "One I would like to spend time getting to know." He kissed her other cheek.

Her senses reeled as he placed feathery-light kisses across the bridge of her nose. Then the import of his words penetrated the happy fog wrapping around her heart. "What are you saying?"

He chuckled. "I'll put it as clearly as possible. I'm in love with you."

"Truly?" She didn't need to ask—the truth shone in his eyes.

"Truly." He leaned toward her, his lips millimeters from hers, then he pulled back. "Don't you have something to say to me?"

Elle raised her eyebrows. "Isn't that a leading question, counsellor?"

"Answer the question," he mock growled, "or you'll be held in contempt of court."

"What would my punishment be?"

He pretended to seriously consider the question. "A kiss every morning and evening."

"That's rather a harsh sentence," she teased.

"Will you answer the question?"

"I believe I will." She waited a beat then added, "I'm in love with you too."

"I was almost hoping you'd pay the fine instead." He grinned, bringing his lips in close proximity to hers again.

"If you ask nicely, I might be persuaded to indulge you."

Elle caught her breath as he lowered his lips to hers. With a sigh, she wrapped her arms around his neck, a feeling of contentment washing over her. Finally, her own happy ending at last.

* * * * *

If you liked this story from Sarah Hamaker,
check out her previous
Love Inspired Suspense book:

Dangerous Christmas Memories

Available from Love Inspired Suspense!
Find more great reads at
www.LoveInspired.com

Dear Reader,

What are you searching for? That was the question circling my mind as I wrote *Vanished Without a Trace*. Most of us are seeking something—answers to prayers, someone or something from our past, or just where we'd set down our favorite mug of tea. Many of us easily find what we're looking for, but at other times, the searching goes on for days, weeks, months, or years. We might not be trying to find a missing person, like Henderson Parker and Elle Updike are in this story, but we're searching just the same.

As Henderson and Elle discover, our searching always goes better when we include God. Whether it's praying for direction or remembering who's in ultimate control of the outcome, keeping God at the forefront of our searching means we will reach a better conclusion than going it alone. Wherever you're seeking, I pray that God will direct your path.

Sarah Hamaker

Get 4 FREE REWARDS!

We'll send you 2 FREE Books plus 2 FREE Mystery Gifts.

FREE
Value Over
$20

Both the **Love Inspired®** and **Love Inspired® Suspense** series feature compelling novels filled with inspirational romance, faith, forgiveness, and hope.

YES! Please send me 2 FREE novels from the Love Inspired or Love Inspired Suspense series and my 2 FREE gifts (gifts are worth about $10 retail). After receiving them, if I don't wish to receive any more books, I can return the shipping statement marked "cancel." If I don't cancel, I will receive 6 brand-new Love Inspired Larger-Print books or Love Inspired Suspense Larger-Print books every month and be billed just $5.99 each in the U.S. or $6.24 each in Canada. That is a savings of at least 17% off the cover price. It's quite a bargain! Shipping and handling is just 50¢ per book in the U.S. and $1.25 per book in Canada.* I understand that accepting the 2 free books and gifts places me under no obligation to buy anything. I can always return a shipment and cancel at any time. The free books and gifts are mine to keep no matter what I decide.

Choose one: ☐ **Love Inspired**
Larger-Print
(122/322 IDN GNWC)

☐ **Love Inspired Suspense**
Larger-Print
(107/307 IDN GNWN)

Name (please print)

Address   Apt. #

City   State/Province   Zip/Postal Code

Email: Please check this box ☐ if you would like to receive newsletters and promotional emails from Harlequin Enterprises ULC and its affiliates. You can unsubscribe anytime.

Mail to the **Harlequin Reader Service:**
IN U.S.A.: P.O. Box 1341, Buffalo, NY 14240-8531
IN CANADA: P.O. Box 603, Fort Erie, Ontario L2A 5X3

Want to try 2 free books from another series! Call 1-800-873-8635 or visit www.ReaderService.com.

*Terms and prices subject to change without notice. Prices do not include sales taxes, which will be charged (if applicable) based on your state or country of residence. Canadian residents will be charged applicable taxes. Offer not valid in Quebec. This offer is limited to one order per household. Books received may not be as shown. Not valid for current subscribers to the Love Inspired or Love Inspired Suspense series. All orders subject to approval. Credit or debit balances in a customer's account(s) may be offset by any other outstanding balance owed by or to the customer. Please allow 4 to 6 weeks for delivery. Offer available while quantities last.

Your Privacy—Your information is being collected by Harlequin Enterprises ULC, operating as Harlequin Reader Service. For a complete summary of the information we collect, how we use this information and to whom it is disclosed, please visit our privacy notice located at corporate.harlequin.com/privacy-notice. From time to time we may also exchange your personal information with reputable third parties. If you wish to opt out of this sharing of your personal information, please visit readerservice.com/consumerschoice or call 1-800-873-8635. **Notice to California Residents**—Under California law, you have specific rights to control and access your data. For more information on these rights and how to exercise them, visit corporate.harlequin.com/california-privacy.

LIRLIS22

Get 4 FREE REWARDS!

We'll send you 2 FREE Books plus <u>2</u> FREE Mystery Gifts.

FREE Value Over **$20**

Both the **Harlequin® Special Edition** and **Harlequin® Heartwarming™** series feature compelling novels filled with stories of love and strength where the bonds of friendship, family and community unite.

YES! Please send me 2 FREE novels from the Harlequin Special Edition or Harlequin Heartwarming series and my 2 FREE gifts (gifts are worth about $10 retail). After receiving them, if I don't wish to receive any more books, I can return the shipping statement marked "cancel." If I don't cancel, I will receive 6 brand-new Harlequin Special Edition books every month and be billed just $4.99 each in the U.S or $5.74 each in Canada, a savings of at least 17% off the cover price or 4 brand-new Harlequin Heartwarming Larger-Print books every month and be billed just $5.74 each in the U.S. or $6.24 each in Canada, a savings of at least 21% off the cover price. It's quite a bargain! Shipping and handling is just 50¢ per book in the U.S. and $1.25 per book in Canada.* I understand that accepting the 2 free books and gifts places me under no obligation to buy anything. I can always return a shipment and cancel at any time. The free books and gifts are mine to keep no matter what I decide.

Choose one: ☐ **Harlequin Special Edition**
(235/335 HDN GNMP)
☐ **Harlequin Heartwarming Larger-Print**
(161/361 HDN GNPZ)

Name (please print)

Address   Apt. #

City   State/Province   Zip/Postal Code

Email: Please check this box ☐ if you would like to receive newsletters and promotional emails from Harlequin Enterprises ULC and its affiliates. You can unsubscribe anytime.

Mail to the **Harlequin Reader Service:**
IN U.S.A.: P.O. Box 1341, Buffalo, NY 14240-8531
IN CANADA: P.O. Box 603, Fort Erie, Ontario L2A 5X3

Want to try 2 free books from another series! Call 1-800-873-8635 or visit www.ReaderService.com.

HSEHW22

COUNTRY LEGACY COLLECTION

19 FREE BOOKS IN ALL!

Cowboys, adventure and romance await you in this new collection! Enjoy superb reading all year long with books by bestselling authors like Diana Palmer, Sasha Summers and Marie Ferrarella!

Visit
ReaderService.com
Today!

**As a valued member of the
Harlequin Reader Service,
you'll find these benefits and more at
ReaderService.com:**

- Try 2 free books from any series
- Access risk-free special offers
- View your account history & manage payments
- Browse the latest Bonus Bucks catalog

Don't miss out!

If you want to stay up-to-date on the latest at the Harlequin
Reader Service and enjoy more content, make sure you've
signed up for our monthly News & Notes email newsletter.
Sign up online at ReaderService.com or by calling Customer
Service at 1-800-873-8635.